Charles W. Eves, Laurence R. Fyfe, Augustus C. Sinclair,
Colonial and Indian Exhibition

Jamaica at the Colonial and Indian Exhibition, London, 1886

Charles W. Eves, Laurence R. Fyfe, Augustus C. Sinclair, Colonial and Indian
Exhibition

Jamaica at the Colonial and Indian Exhibition, London, 1886

ISBN/EAN: 9783337330064

Printed in Europe, USA, Canada, Australia, Japan

Cover: Foto ©Andreas Hilbeck / pixelio.de

More available books at **www.hansebooks.com**

JAMAICA

AT THE

Colonial and Indian Exhibition,

LONDON, 1886.

" Jamaica's beauteous isle and genial clime
I sing. Attend, ye Britons ! nor disdain
Th' adventurous muse to verdant vales that soars,
And radiant realms, beyond th' Atlantic wave ;
Ardent to gather for her Albion's brow
A tropic wreath, green with immortal spring."

BRYAN EDWARDS.

Honorary Commissioner in London:

C. WASHINGTON EVES, Esq.

Commission at Jamaica:

REV. DR. ROBB, D.D., *Chairman.*

DR. J. C. PHILLIPPO.   HON. H. J. KEMBLE.

HON. C. B. MOSSE, C.B. &c.   R. H. B. HOTCHKIN, ESQ., M.A.

THE REV. JOHN RADCLIFFE.

H. PRIEST, *Secretary.*

PRINTED BY
SPOTTISWOODE AND CO., NEW-STREET SQUARE
LONDON

WHEN practical arrangements for the representation of the Colonies at the Exhibition were being made, the West Indian industries were in a state of considerable depression, and it was doubtful whether any such appearance could be made as would be entirely satisfactory in itself or pleasurable to remember. But the encouragement given by His Royal Highness the Prince of Wales, who is ever ready to view with kindly consideration all the efforts towards progress made in any portion of the outlying dominions of his mother, the Queen-Empress, induced the West India Colonies to come to the front, and to avail themselves of that which might be truly called the opportunity of a century. The visit of the Royal Princes, sons of the Prince of Wales, also tended to strengthen the wish to be well represented in the old country; and when the record of that visit gave prominence to the feelings of pride in the victories of Rodney and other gallant sailors and soldiers who fought for England at a time when the West Indian seas were the arena of the great nations of Europe, the desire of being recognised as having an important share in the glorious past of England became more intensified. At the same time, more practical considerations conduced to the same end. These colonies produce articles of food and luxury which the world consumes without thinking of the places of production, the people engaged in tropical industries, and the peculiar conditions under which these industries exist. To bring producer and consumer, therefore, together, to make them, if only for a time, sympathise with and understand each other, to get them to discuss their mutual obligations, and to forget the blunders and prejudices of byegone years, would lead, not only to more cordial sentiments, but to what is perhaps more important, increased and more prosperous trade. From the time that Pitt awed a tumultuous House of Commons by crying, in stentorian tones, "Sugar! Sugar! Sugar!" down to the much changed conditions of the present time, the fortunes of the West Indies have been largely concerned with the position in the markets of the world of that article which a recent Chancellor of the Exchequer described as "the delight of youth and the solace of age." The tropical planter wishes to convince his sugar-eating brother at home that the produce of the cane is infinitely superior in sweetness and nutritive qualities to the sickly stuff obtained from bounty-feed beet on the Continent of Europe. This understanding is likely to come about. There are other products in the West Indies besides sugar, as we shall see later on. And the mere fact of becoming acquainted, through pictures, photographs, and natural objects, with the beautiful scenery and interesting curiosities, appealing to the imagination of the general observer, the scientific thought of the ethnological student, and the large-heartedness of the philanthropist, cannot fail to widen the horizon of the insular English mind, and perhaps impress it with new suggestions of duty. Trade and commerce are, after all, the practical results of sentiment, and it is into the aspect of buyer and seller, of giving employment to English ships and English labour, and of affording outlets to English capital, that the whole question finally resolves itself.

In this scene of Imperial fraternisation, Jamaica plays an important part. This Colony has always had a peculiar interest for the people of England. Its acquisition by Cromwell, the influence upon it of the naval and military operations of the succeeding 150 years, the rise of its prosperity, the slave trade and slavery, the effect of that social revolution known as emancipation, and the hopes entertained of the upward progress of the negro race—the peculiar exclusiveness of the old protective or " Colonial" system, the abandonment of this and the havoc caused by the admission into Great Britain on equal terms of foreign slave-grown sugar, the decline of the sugar industry, the forming of provision grounds, and the attention paid to the cultivation of other products—the long reign of the House of Assembly, until the riots of 1865 led to the abolition of Representative Government—the 18 years of Crown Government, and the new elective constitution under which the Colony is now placed as the result of Lord Derby's "new departure"—all these points constitute an historical record of no mean interest; they explain the concern felt for the Colony by Englishmen in the past, and they afford a ground for a new and larger sympathy in the future. Nor, in forecasting what is to come, must we forget the likelihood of its again becoming a great entrepôt of commerce when the Panama Canal, which is to unite two oceans and divert a large part of the sea traffic of the world, is an accomplished fact. Its perennial beauty and varied climate must make it in time a health resort for Europe and America, and the Laureate might have had some picture of the Jamaica hills in his mind when he wrote the following lines, which, although they may not be entirely accurate in detail, and although they miss some of the most delightful characteristics of the island, namely, its rivers, its picturesque ravines, and its many streams, may stand as a suggestion in outline of a tropical scene :—

" The mountain wooded to the peak ; the lawns
And winding glades high up like ways to heaven ;
The slender coco's drooping crown of plumes ;
The lightning flash of insect and of bird ;
The lustre of the long convolvuluses
That coiled around the stately stems and ran
Even to the limit of the land ; the glows
And glories of the broad belt of the world."

Turning from these general considerations to a few words of practical explanation, it is necessary to state how the Jamaica people carried out their wish to be represented at the Exhibition. The Legislature necessarily had to vote a certain sum of money. The exhibits were collected in the island and forwarded by "The Institute of Jamaica," an admirable and well-managed Society, established by law, and one of whose duties it is "to provide for the holding of exhibitions illustrative of the Industries of Jamaica." It has charge of the museum, and indeed carries out the functions of the former "Royal Society of Arts and Agriculture," which exercised much influence in its time. Cordial assistance was also given in the collection of exhibits by Mr. D. Morris, himself a Governor of the Institute, as well as the head of the Botanic Gardens. This gentleman is now the Assistant-Director of Kew Gardens, and, since his recent arrival in England, has taken much interest in the Court. On April 10, 1886, I was appointed by His Excellency Sir Henry Norman, the Governor of the Colony, with the concurrence of the Jamaica Institute, to the important office of Honorary Commissioner for Jamaica at the Colonial and Indian Exhibition. I have gladly devoted much time to the arrangement of the exhibits sent from the Colony and others collected by me in England, and, when not present myself, have always had a representative in the Court, to give explanations to visitors. On May 1, the Prince of Wales paid an official visit to the Exhibition, and in examining the Jamaica Court, His Royal Highness expressed himself as highly satisfied with its appearance. The Queen, upon her visit on May 21, was also graciously pleased to express her interest and approbation.

Subsequent to the arrival of the exhibits from the Colony, there came a large number of copies of the "Handbook compiled for the Governors of the Jamaica Institute, by Laurence R. Fyfe and A. C. Sinclair, compilers of the Official Handbook of Jamaica." Accompanying these were copies of a detailed catalogue of all the articles sent for exhibition. These papers, so full of valuable information in regard to

JAMAICA. FRONT VIEW OF THE COURT.

the history, condition and products of the Colony, were distributed and the copies soon exhausted. It was therefore thought desirable by me to reprint them, and place them together in one volume, with such particulars regarding the Court itself as might serve as a kind of general guide to visitors. I therefore hope that this book, which will be distributed gratuitously, will meet with the approval of His Excellency the Governor and the Governors of the Jamaica Institute, and will not only serve a temporary purpose but will constitute a permanent record of the Jamaica Court, such as may be referred to with pleasure by all who are interested in Jamaica, and keep alive for many years to come, so far as this island is concerned, the memory of the Colonial and Indian Exhibition of 1886.

The front view of the Court, as well as that looking towards the south, photographs of which are here reproduced, will give a general idea of its appearance. But the real usefulness of the Exhibition can only be understood after a detailed inspection. Philosophers tell us that the two great powers of the human mind are observation and reflection, and that, the mental powers being limited, these two operations cannot take place at the same time. The advantage, therefore, of a written record is, that it assists the memory, stored by observation, and gives fulness to a permanent impression, the completeness of which would not be " edged off " by time. The list of exhibits from the Colony, and the supplementary list of articles, will be useful to the planter and merchant, to the shipper of English goods, who wishes to know what he can get in exchange, and to the colonial exporter who has the varied products of the island to draw upon for English and European consumption. As an economic and commercial study, therefore, as well as an attempted blending of form and colour to constitute a picture, the Court may be regarded. Of course, one may see orange trees in public gardens and in many other places in England, but the orange tree at the right entrance of the Jamaica Court represents what will be an important Jamaica industry. The visitor to the United States will probably find on his breakfast and dinner tables the oranges from Florida, but the crop there is subject to a touch of frost which cannot be experienced in Jamaica, and a large trade is possible from the Colony in this fruit. Oranges and other West Indian fruit can be had in England, thanks to the admirable arrangements for conveyance made by that enterprising firm, Scrutton, Sons & Co., whose recent importation of these products, under conditions of special advantage in their steamers, was a great success, and holds out much promise for the future. The Jamaica orange should be well known in England, if more extensive cultivation of it be entered upon. The aloe on the left hand of the Court, the palms and ferns distributed throughout, refresh the eye and fill the mind with pictures of tropical vegetation. Art is interspersed with nature. On the left are to be seen large oil paintings of Jamaica scenes. The first is the principal street in Kingston as it appeared at the beginning of this century. The military uniforms, the planter's dress, the general appearance of the street, are all characteristic of the time and place. Next hangs a portrait of the present Governor, General Sir Henry Norman, which will be recognised at once by those who know His Excellency. Then another large oil painting arrests attention, with its view of Montego Bay, and its effects of sky and sea.

A splendid turtle back, surmounted by the arms of the colony, which are set off with grass plumes and fan decoration, remind the visitor in what part of the Empire he now stands. The pictures on this wall close with another large oil painting, representing a general view of Kingston and Port Royal, and the long stretch of sand known as the Palisades. Turning round from this picture, another oil painting on the opposite side, recalling one of the most beautiful scenes in Jamaica, Bog Walk, will be noticed, and, looking up, surmounting the centre arches of the Court on the inside, two more oil paintings of scenery are visible, the one to the left being Stewart

Bluff, on the north side of Jamaica, and the other being the Coast of Green Island.

In the open arches at the back of the Court two other large oil paintings are placed, one representing Holland Estate, St. Thomas, and the other Port Maria. These paintings are of quite modern execution, but they are faithful representations of the scenes they purport to reproduce. In the front of the arch hangs the portrait of the Earl of Balcarres, who was Governor of Jamaica from 1795 to 1801, lent by the present head of the family. Numerous photographs, old Jamaica newspapers riddled with worm holes and yellow with their eighty years of age, and the specimens of lace bark with which the lower parts of the stands are decorated, may be noticed in passing; but, turning to natural products, a prominent trophy in the front centre of the Court is the Rum for which Jamaica is so famous. In handsome glass jars, this spirit, which has been designated "liquid sunshine," from the fact that it is the immediate and natural product of the cane, is shown from the uncoloured white to the deepest shades. All the well-known marks are here represented, as well as the crops of different years. The row of sugars contains some fine specimens, although from many causes Jamaica is not now the great sugar colony that it was, say, in Monk Lewis's time, 100 years ago. Besides producing sugar and rum, Jamaica is a large fruit-growing country, as suggested above, a ready market being found in the United States, and probably also in England, for oranges, shaddocks, and bananas. A number of other important industries are also represented in this Court. The display of coffee is especially fine, occupying a large space on the centre stand facing the entrance. The cocoa, pimento, pepper, annatto are all suggestive of Nature's bounty, in providing useful things to make human life more pleasant; and not the least important of these means of amelioration is to be found in the cinchona bark, of which quinine is made, so largely shown in this Court. Standing in front of the Court, and looking at it as a whole, the effect is very pleasing. The suspended alligator at the back, the case of humming birds, the shark with his attendant small fish, the two piles of rum casks reaching high up, the stands of sugar canes, the variegated woods, the hammocks overhead, the dried turtle case, and the boxes of Jamaica cigars, the barrels of Turk's Island salt, the hats with their broad brims shading from the tropical sun, the pressed leaves of ferns, the case of bonnets, baskets and fancy work shown by the Women's Self-Help Society of Kingston, the general arrangement of palms, mahogany plants, ferns, grasses, and other foliage, make up a picture which, studied generally or in detail, cannot fail to be regarded with interest by Englishmen, whether resident at home or on a visit from the island. The secret of any success obtained is, of course, to be found in the intrinsic interest of the exhibits and their adaptability for effective grouping.

The visitor should also see the admirable collection of Jamaica coffees, forwarded by Messrs. Brancker, Boxwell and Co., of Liverpool. This collection is part of the economic food display on the left hand side of the Indian Court, starting from the Jungle end.

Upon the whole, a very complete exposition is given of the produce of Jamaica. But this suggests what a large increase of cultivation is possible. The planting of cacao is practically beginning. The cinchona plants present a good appearance, but the industry is yet in its infancy. Bananas, the principal fruit industry of the island, are exported to the value of £200,000. These are largely consumed and much appreciated in the United States. The pine-apple, too, is capable of a much larger export. Jamaica tea, of good flavour, would find a ready market in London. There is, indeed, no early limit to the production of these articles. But the great requisite is colonists. Young men with a small capital, and sufficient resources to enable them to wait until the trees bear (which may be from four to six years), would find a competence in this colony in the cultivation of cinchona or coffee. A Jamaica Governor, some six or seven years ago, invested in a coffee plantation, and it is understood that he is beginning to receive the reward of his enterprise. A special feature of Jamaica, too, is the pens. These are extensive sweeps of land for growing grass for the rearing of cattle. The large population of Jamaica ought to eat more beef. An old Jamaica colonist used to say that if the population would eat more animal food, civilisation would make greater strides. However this may be, pen-keeping has not been unprofitable, and has been engaged in by young Englishmen who are fond of an open air life, who are accustomed to horsemanship, and who at the same time like to put money in their pockets. Of course, the sale of cattle depends upon the demand arising from the sugar estates for draught purposes as well as for food. The sugar cultivation has been stationary, at a comparatively low figure, for many years, but with a turn in the market and perhaps a countervailing duty on bounty fed beet sugar imported into Great Britain (which is certainly more within the bounds of possibility than many people imagine) there would be reason to hope for an extension of cultivation. The German bounties will certainly be reduced by a kind of sliding scale during the next two years. It may be interesting to place on record the recent German legislation on this important subject :— "NEW GERMAN LAW.—Tax on roots, 1 mark, 70 pf. Drawback from August 1st, 1886, to 30th September, 1887, m. 18. From October 1887, m. 17.25. For loaf sugar, m. 22.20 to October 31st, 1887 ; and after, m. 21.56. This law continues the principle of the tax on roots, and it shows a desire to export white sugars for direct consumption. At the usual computation of 1,000 kilos. per ton, and 20 marks to the £, the bounty will be reduced from 36s. as at present, after October 1886, to 27s., and after October 1887 to 19s. 6d., at 9 tons beet to 1 sugar ; and from 20s. to 2s. 6d. at 10 tons. It takes on the average 9½ tons roots to make 1 ton sugar in Germany." A new law has also been passed in France increasing the fiscal advantage enjoyed by French colonial sugar on its importation into France, but otherwise continuing the law of 1884, which provides for the next three years a gradually increasing yield of sugar from the weight of beet roots worked in the factories. Upon the whole there is movement in this Bounty question, and it may be hoped that within a reasonable time the system may be discontinued either by the voluntary action of foreign Governments, or by practical measures on the part of the English Government to remove the bounty, for the benefit of the English revenue, upon the entrance of such sugar into English ports. It should be added that negotiations have recently taken place between Jamaica and Canada, and also with the United States, for a reciprocal trade arrangement, but these have not yet produced any result, although such result is certainly within the range of "practical politics."

Jamaica, as a field for agricultural enterprise by Englishmen, is open to many settlers. The Government will, no doubt, give all information as to the acquisition of suitable land. For labourers, whose services are necessary in all agricultural undertakings, it offers opportunities. The East Indian coolie is there earning his shilling a day instead of his two annas in India. The saving Chinaman adapts himself first to labour in the fields or factories, and afterwards makes money as a pedlar or petty tradesman; the indigenous black man (for so he may now be called) is cultivating his provision ground and keeping his family together by the sale of the produce, or he is off to take part in the work of the Panama Canal—a proceeding not always to his own health or advantage. In point of fact there is room for enterprising small capitalists from Europe; and although labour may be somewhat shifting and uncertain in different parts, such difficulties could be overcome, and in course of time it may be hoped that this island will be recognised as an attractive centre of agricultural and commercial enterprise, and its past difficulties be forgotten in the dawn of that brighter era for which its capabilities are so eminently adapted.

1 FEN COURT,
LONDON : *July* 1886.   C. WASHINGTON EVES.

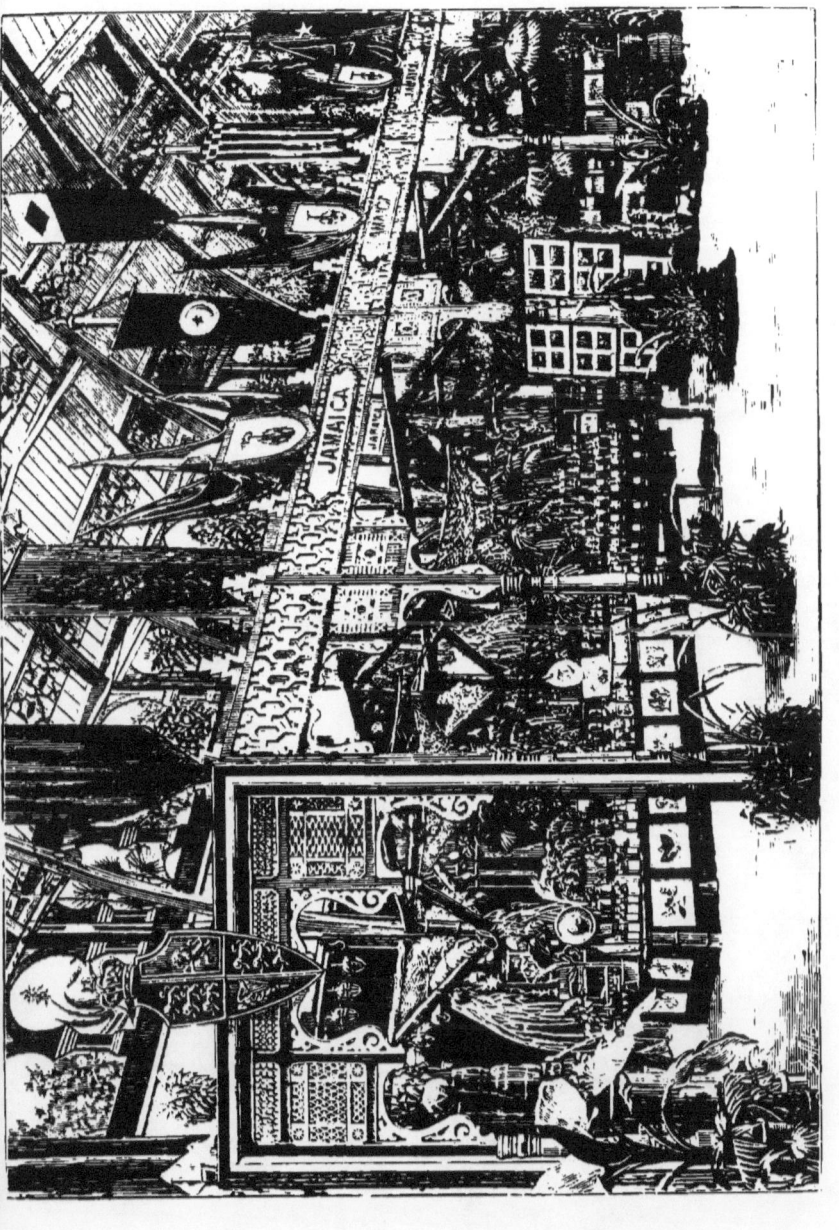

JAMAICA: LOOKING TOWARDS THE SOUTH.

CATALOGUE OF ARTICLES FORWARDED

FROM THE

ISLAND OF JAMAICA.

———••••••••———

JAMAICA is the largest and most valuable of the West India Islands belonging to Great Britain, and it has been termed "one of the brightest jewels in the British Crown." Its greatest length is 144 miles, and it contains 4,200 square miles. The value of the exports during the year 1885 was £1,408,848; of the imports, £1,487,833; and the revenue, £545,000.

The chief exports in order of importance are—Sugar, £307,826; Rum, £234,053; Tropical Fruits, £181,501; Coffee, £157,281; Dye Woods, £155,526; Pimento, £53,867; Ginger, £20,168; Beeswax and Honey, £7,775; Cacao, £6,359; Lance Wood Spars, £2,005, &c., &c.

As regards distribution of trade, the produce of the island shipped in 1885 was as follows—United Kingdom, 37·2 per cent.; United States of America, 42·2 per cent.; Dominion of Canada, 5·4 per cent.; all other countries, 15·2 per cent.

The surface of the island is greatly diversified, and hence it affords means for the cultivation of most economic tropical plants from sea-level to an elevation of 7,000 feet. Cattle and horse-raising are important industries on the northern slopes of the island where the nutritious Guinea grass affords excellent pasture all the year round.

The climate of Jamaica is superior to that of any of the West India Islands, and in the hills especially, at moderate elevation, it is recommended as eminently suitable to northern people obliged to seek a mild health resort during the winter months.

The population of Jamaica by last census was 580,000, being an increase of 73,650 during the previous ten years. Of these there are—whites, 14,432; coloured, 109,946; black, 444,186; the remainder being Coolies and Chinese.

The Government is administered by a Governor appointed by the Crown, assisted by a Legislative Council composed of nominated and elected members, the latter having the majority.

Fuller information respecting Jamaica may be obtained from " The Handbook of Jamaica," an octavo volume of some 500 pages, published annually under the auspices of government, and which is a most complete repository for everything connected with the island. The volume for 1885-86 is published by Edward Stanford, 53 Charing Cross, London.

I.—SUGAR.

The export of sugar from Jamaica in 1885 was 24,985 tons, of the value of £307,826. This, combined with rum, renders the produce of the sugar-cane the staple industry of the island. The general depression in the price of sugar is felt in Jamaica as in all sugar-producing countries.

1. Vacuum pan sugar (white), Bushy Park, Louis Verley.
2. Vacuum pan sugar (yellow), Bushy Park, Louis Verley.
3. Vacuum pan sugar, Bushy Park, Louis Verley.
4. Vacuum pan sugar (white), Ewing's Caymanas, J. Crum-Ewing.
5. Vacuum pan sugar (yellow), Ewing's Caymanas, J. Crum-Ewing.
6. Centrifugal sugar, Greenwich Estate, C. J. Ward.
7. Centrifugal sugar, Moneymusk Estate, C. J. Ward.
8. Centrifugal sugar, Seven Plantations, J. Grenan.
9. Centrifugal sugar, Vale-Royal, Hon. Henry Sewell.
10. Centrifugal sugar, Arcadia, Hon. Henry Sewell.
11. Muscovado sugar, Savoy Estate, J. W. Kemp.
12. Muscovado sugar, Whitney Estate, E. C. Elliott.
13. Muscovado sugar, Mona Estate, Louis Verley.
14. Muscovado sugar, Y. S., C. W. Treleaven.
15. Muscovado sugar, Lloyds, George Stiebel.
16. Muscovado sugar, Worthy Park, J. Gray.
17. Muscovado sugar, Hyde Hall, L. C. Shirley.
18. Muscovado sugar, Etingdon, L. C. Shirley.
19. Muscovado sugar (Ranger cured), Bogue, C. W. Treleaven.
20. Muscovado sugar, George Solomon & Co.

II.—RUM.

During the year 1885, Jamaica rum was exported to the extent of 2,080,471 gallons, of the value of £234,053. This industry occupies so prominent a position, and is so widely known, that it is needless to enlarge upon it. The exhibits include the finest and best brands produced in the island, and embrace estates and merchants' rums of acknowledged excellence.

(A.)—Estates Rum.

21. Crop, 1885, Lancaster Estate	.	C. H. W. Gordon.
22. Crop, 1885, Hyde Estate .	.	Hon. Henry Sewell.
23. Crop, 1885, Steelfield Estate.	.	Hon. Henry Sewell.
24. Crop, 1885, Vale Royal Estate	.	Hon. Henry Sewell.
25. Crop, 1885, Lottery Estate .	.	Hon. Henry Sewell.

26.	Crop, 1885, Oxford Estate	. . . .	C. J. M. Barrett.
27.	Crop, 1885, Braco Estate	. . . .	C. H. W. Gordon.
28.	Crop, 1885, Cambridge Estate	. . .	Mrs. E. Thompson.
29.	Crop, 1885 (white), Lodge Estate.	. . .	H. J. Ronaldson.
30.	Crop, 1885 (white), Lodge Estate.	. . .	H. J. Ronaldson.
31.	Crop, 1885, Lodge Estate	. . . .	H. J. Ronaldson.
32.	Crop, 1885, Chester Estate .	. . .	A. B. Gentles.
33.	Crop, 1885, Fontabelle Estate	. . .	C. H. Stewart.
34.	Crop, 1885, Brampton Bryan Estate	. .	Dr. Proctor.
35.	Crop, 1885, Georgia Estate .	. . .	J. W. Gordon.
36.	Crop, 1885, Bryan Castle Estate .	. .	Dr. Proctor.
37.	Crop, 1885, Lloyds' Estate .	. . .	George Stiebel.
38.	Crop, 1885, Content Estate .	. . .	C. N. Sterling.
39.	Crop, 1886, Savoy Estate	. . . .	J. W. Kemp.
40.	Crop, 1882, Spring Estate	. . . .	Walter Ogilvy.
41.	Crop, 1885, Spring Estate	. . . .	Walter Ogilvy.
42.	Crop, 1885, Hopewell Estate	. . .	Walter Ogilvy.
43.	Crop, 1885 (white), Hopewell Estate	. .	Walter Ogilvy.
44.	Crop, 1885, Hordley Estate .	. . .	J. Harrison.
45.	Crop, 1885, Amity Hall Estate	. . .	J. Harrison.
46.	Crop, 1864, Hordley Estate .	. . .	J. Harrison.
47.	Crop, 1886, Tulloch Estate .	. . :	J. McPhail.
48.	Crop, 1886 (white), Tulloch Estate	. .	J. McPhail.
49.	Crop, 1885, Knollis Estate .	. . .	J. McPhail.
50.	Crop, 1886, Y. S. Estate	. . .	C. W. Treleaven.
51.	Crop, 1886, Ipswich Estate .	. . .	C. W. Treleaven.
52.	Crop, 1886, Bogue Estate	. . .	C. W. Treleaven.
53.	Crop, 1863, Friendship Estate	. . .	C. W. Eves & Co.
54.	Crop, 1867 (white), Friendship Estate.	. .	C. W. Eves.
55.	Crop, 1868, Friendship Estate	. . .	C. W. Eves & Co.
56.	Crop, 1870, Friendship Estate	. . .	C. W. Eves & Co.
57.	Crop, 1872, Friendship Estate	. . .	C. W. Eves & Co.
58.	Crop, 1874, Friendship Estate	. . .	C. W. Eves & Co.
59.	Crop, 1876, Friendship Estate	. . .	C. W. Eves & Co.
60.	Crop, 1878, Friendship Estate	. . .	C. W. Eves & Co.
61.	Crop, 1880, Friendship Estate	. . .	C. W. Eves & Co.
62.	Crop, 1882, Friendship Estate	. . .	C. W. Eves & Co.
63.	Crop, 1882 (white), Friendship Estate	. .	C. W. Eves & Co.
64.	Crop, 1883, Friendship Estate	. . .	C. W. Eves & Co.
65.	Crop, 1885, Friendship Estate	. . .	C. W. Eves & Co.
66.	Crop, 1886, Friendship Estate	. . .	C. W. Eves & Co.
67.	Crop, 1886, Cornwall Estate	. . .	Col. F. Lushington.
68.	Crop, 1886, Blackheath Estate	. . .	Eustace Grieg.
69.	Crop, 1886, Blue Castle Estate	. . .	Eustace Grieg.
70.	Crop, 1886, Golden Grove Estate .	. .	De B. S. Heaven.
71.	Crop, 1886, Halse Hall Estate	. . .	J. J. Ronaldson.
72.	Crop, 1885, Moneymusk Estate .	. .	C. J. Ward.
73.	Crop, 1885, Greenwich Estate	. . .	C. J. Ward.
74.	Crop, 1886, Worthy Park Estate .	. .	Col. Talbot.
75.	Crop, 1886, Park Hall Estate	. . .	H. T. Ronaldson.
76.	Crop, 1885, Mona Estate	. . . .	Louis Verley.
77.	Crop, 1885 (white), Mona Estate.	. . .	Louis Verley.
78.	Crop, 1885, Bushy Park Estate	. . .	Louis Verley.
79.	Crop, 1885 (white), Bushy Park Estate	. .	Louis Verley.
80.	Crop, 1886, Etingdon Estate	. . .	L. C. Shirley.
81.	Crop, 1886, Hyde Hall Estate	. . .	L. C. Shirley.
82.	Crop, 1886, Kent Estate	. . . .	Hon. W. Kerr.

83.	Crop, 1886, Gales Valley Estate	Hon. W. Kerr.
84.	Crop, 1886, Telston Estate	Hon. W. Kerr.
85.	Crop. 1886, Golden Grove Estate . . .	Hon. W. Kerr.
86.	Crop, 1886, Wiltshire Estate	Hon. W. Kerr.
87.	Crop, 1876 (10 years old), Orange Valley Estate.	Hon. W. Kerr.
88.	Crop, 1886, Orange Valley Estate . . .	Hon. W. Kerr.
89.	Crop, 1886, Catherine Hall Estate . . .	Hon. W. Kerr.
90.	Crop, 1886, Guilsbro' Estate	Hon. W. Kerr.
91.	Crop, 1886, Round Hill Estate	Hon. W. Kerr.
92.	Crop, 1886, Dundee Estate	Hon. W. Kerr.
93.	Crop, 1886, Cherry Garden Estate . . .	C. A. Robinson.
94.	Crop, 1886 (white), Cherry Garden Estate . .	C. A. Robinson.

(B.)—Merchants' Rum.

95.	Table rum, Crop, 1885 . . .	J. M. Farquharson.
96.	Table rum, Crop, 1875 . .	J. M. Farquharson.
97.	Rum, 1 year old . .	D. Finzi & Co.
98.	Rum, 5 years old . .	D. Finzi & Co.
99.	Rum, 10 years old . .	D. Finzi & Co.
100.	Rum, 15 years old .	D. Finzi & Co.
101.	Rum, 20 years old .	D. Finzi & Co.
102.	Rum, 31 years old .	D. Finzi & Co.
103.	Rum, 10 years old .	Wray & Nephew.
104.	Rum, 15 years old .	Wray & Nephew.
105.	Rum, 25 years old .	Wray & Nephew.
106.	Rum, (old) . . .	Simon & Le Ray.
107.	Rum (white) . .	Simon & Le Ray.
108.	Rum (very old) . .	P. Desnoes & Son.
109.	Rum (white) . .	P. Desnoes & Son.

III.—LIQUEURS, CORDIALS, &c.

110.	Sweet orange spirit . . .	S. T. Scharschmidt, Mandeville.
111.	Seville orange spirit . . .	S. T. Scharschmidt, Mandeville.
112.	Sweet orange wine . . .	S. T. Scharschmidt, Mandeville.
113.	Orange wine	Wray & Nephew, Kingston.
114.	Orange wine (white)	Wray & Nephew, Kingston.
115.	Ginger wine	Wray & Nephew, Kingston.
116.	Ginger wine (white)	Wray & Nephew, Kingston.
117.	Pimento Dram	Wray & Nephew, Kingston.
118.	Prune Dram	Wray & Nephew, Kingston.
119.	Bitters	Wray & Nephew, Kingston.
120.	Crème de Noyau	Wray & Nephew, Kingston.
121.	Quinine bitters	Delgado Brothers, Falmouth.
122.	Rum shrub	Simon & Le Ray, Kingston.
123.	Cashew wine	Simon & Le Ray, Kingston.
124.	Pimento cordial	Simon & Le Ray, Kingston.
125.	White ginger wine	Simon & Le Ray, Kingston.
126.	White ginger cordial. . . .	Simon & Le Ray, Kingston.
127.	White orange wine	Simon & Le Ray, Kingston.
128.	Pure orange cordial	Simon & Le Ray, Kingston.
129.	Pure orange wine	Simon & Le Ray, Kingston.
130.	Liqueur d'Or	Simon & Le Ray, Kingston.
131.	Rosolio	Simon & Le Ray, Kingston.

5

132.	Stomachic bitters	. .	Simon & Le Ray, Kingston.
133.	Bitters	. . . .	Simon & Le Ray, Kingston.
134.	White peppermint wine	.	Simon & Le Ray, Kingston.
136.	Prune bark cordial	. .	Simon & Le Ray, Kingston.
137.	Bitterine	. . . .	Simon & Le Ray, Kingston.
138.	Crème de Noyau (pink)	.	Simon & Le Ray, Kingston.
139.	Crème de Noyau (white)	.	Simon & Le Ray, Kingston.
140.	White ginger wine	. .	P. Desnoes & Son, Kingston.
141.	Ginger wine	. . .	P. Desnoes & Son, Kingston.
142.	Orange wine	. . .	P. Desnoes & Son, Kingston.
143.	Bitters	. . . .	P. Desnoes & Son, Kingston.
144.	Peppermint cordial	. .	P. Desnoes & Son, Kingston.
145.	Pimento Dram	. . .	P. Desnoes & Son, Kingston.
146.	Noyau	. . . .	P. Desnoes & Son, Kingston.
147.	Parfait Amour	. . .	P. Desnoes & Son, Kingston
148.	Rosolio	. . . .	P. Desnoes & Son, Kingston.
149.	Fullermum	. . .	P. Desnoes & Son, Kingston.
150.	Aniseed	. . . .	P. Desnoes & Son Kingston.
151.	Anisado	. . . .	P. Desnoes & Son Kingston.
152.	Orange juice	. . .	P. Desnoes & Son, Kingston.

IV.—TROPICAL FRUITS.

Next to sugar and rum the chief industrial interest in Jamaica, at present, is connected with the raising and shipping of tropical fruits to the United States of America. During the year 1885 fruit to the value of £181,501 was thus exported. Most of this fruit is shipped to the Northern ports of New York, Philadelphia, and Baltimore; but now that the strict quarantine restrictions between Jamaica and New Orleans have been removed, it is hoped that soon a large trade will be established between that port and this island. Up to the present time sufficient attention has not been paid to the packing of fruit— more especially pine-apples and oranges—despatched from Jamaica; and hence the low prices in several cases realised. It is evident, taking into consideration the quality of the fruit which leaves this island, that higher prices could and would be obtained if more care were bestowed upon the wrapping. Oranges, pine-apples, and other fruit have been exported in small quantities to the United Kingdom; but no trade of this nature has been hitherto established.

153.	Caramba (Averrhoa Carambola), Governor's Institute of Jamaica.			
154.	Mango (Mangifera indica var.),	,,	,,	,,
155.	Cashew (Anacardium occidentale),	,,	,,	,,
156.	Star-apple (Chrysophyllum Cainito),	,,	,,	,,
157.	Jimbling (Cicca disticha),	,,	,,	,,
158.	Tree tomato (Cyphomandra betacea),	,,	,,	,,
159.	Nutmegs (Myristica fragrans),	,,	,,	,,
160.	Cocoa-plum (Chrysobalanus Icaco),	,,	,,	
161.	Ginep (Melicocca bijuga),	,,	,,	,,
162.	Walnut (Aleurites triloba),	,,	,,	,,

163. Jew plum (Spondias dulcis), Governor's Institute of Jamaica.
164. Ylang-Ylang (Artobotrys odoratissima), „ „ „
165. Mangoes, No. 11 (Mangifera indica var.), „ „ „
166. Alligator pear (Persea gratissima), „ „ „
167. Alligator pear (purple) (Persea gratissima) „ „
168. Chocho (Sechium edule), „ „ „
169. Akee (Blighia sapida), „ „ „
170. Jamaica peppers (10 varieties), W. M. Bailey, Kingston.
171. Blimbi (Averrhoa Bilimbi), J. J. Bowrey, Kingston.
172. Guava (Psidium Guaiava), J. J. Bowrey, Kingston.

V.—ECONOMIC PRODUCTS of the COCOANUT PALM.
(*Cocos nucifera.*)
173. Ripe nuts.
174. Ripe nuts, dissected to show nut in husk.
175. Ripe nuts, cleared of husk and polished.
176. Small nuts, immature forms.
177. Young plants.
178. Nuts half-husked.
179. Varnished nuts.
180. Unvarnished nuts.
181. Growing nuts.
182. Bunches of ripe nuts.
183. Stems of the cocoanut palm.

(B.)—Exhibited by the General Penitentiary.
184. Doormat of cocoanut fibre.
185. Whitewash brush of cocoanut fibre.
186. Horsebrush of cocoanut fibre.
187. Shoebrushes of cocoanut fibre.
188. Cocoanut fibre.
189. Coatbrush of cocoanut fibre.

VI.—COFFEE.

In Jamaica two very distinct classes of coffee are produced. The total export is about 84,000 cwt. per annum. Of this about 10,000 cwt. is " Blue Mountain Coffee " of the finest quality, consigned almost entirely to the Liverpool market, where it sells from 100/ to 142/ per cwt. The remaining portion of Jamaica coffee is grown chiefly by negro settlers, is badly cured, and hence fetches comparatively low prices.

190. Coffee, Clydesdale Estate . . . . Mrs. MacLaverty.
191. Coffee (in parchment), Clydesdale Estate . . Mrs. MacLaverty.
192. Coffee, Sherwood Forest Estate . . . . John Davidson.
193. Coffee (in husk), Sherwood Forest Estate . . John Davidson.
194. Coffee (in parchment), Sherwood Forest Estate . John Davidson.
195. Coffee (green), Sherwood Forest Estate . . John Davidson.
196. Coffee (peaberry), Sherwood Forest Estate . . John Davidson.
197. Coffee, Portland Gap Estate, Gosset . . . Treleaven & Co.
198. Coffee, Arntully Estate . . . . . W. A. Sabonadière.
199. Coffee (in parchment), Arntully Estate . . W. A. Sabonadière.

200.	Coffee (dried in cherry), Arntully Estate . .	W. A. Sabonadière.
201.	Coffee, Tweedside Estate	Capt. Baker.
202.	Coffee (in parchment), Tweedside Estate . .	Capt. Baker.
203.	Coffee, Langley Estate	W. E. Sant.
204.	Coffee (in parchment), Langley Estate . .	W. E. Sant.
205.	Coffee (in berry), Langley Estate . . .	W. E. Sant.
206.	Coffee, Radnor Estate	J. A. Stephens.
207.	Coffee, Whitfield Hall Estate	De B. S. Heaven.
208.	Coffee, Clifton Mount Estate	John McLean.
208½.	Coffee (peaberry), Clifton Mount Estate . .	John McLean.
209.	Coffee, Petersfield Estate	C. J. Ward.
210.	Coffee (peaberry), Abbey Green Estate . .	C. J. Ward.
211.	Coffee, Abbey Green Estate	C. J. Ward.
212.	Coffee (peaberry), Abbey Green Estate . .	C. J. Ward.
213.	Coffee, Newton Estate	John Hollingsworth.
214.	Coffee, Spring Hill Estate	Rev. J. Seed Roberts.
215.	Coffee (No. 1), Spring Hill Estate . . .	Rev. J. Seed Roberts.
216.	Coffee (in parchment), Spring Hill Estate . .	Rev. J. Seed Roberts.
217.	Coffee (peaberry), Spring Hill Estate . . .	Rev. J. Seed Roberts.
218.	Coffee, Ewings Caymanas Estate	J. Crum-Ewing.
218a.	Coffee, The Cottage Estate	A. W. Kemble.
219.	Coffee, Windsor Forest Estate	S. H. Watson.
220.	Coffee (peaberry), Windsor Forest Estate . .	S. H. Watson.
221.	Coffee, Brokenhurst Estate	Walter H. Wynne.
222.	Coffee (peaberry), Brokenhurst Estate . . .	Walter H. Wynne.
223.	Coffee (parchment), Brokenhurst Estate . .	Walter H. Wynne.
224.	Coffee (peaberry), Brokenhurst Estate . .	Walter H. Wynne.
225.	Coffee (Groves Estate)	C. R. Taylor.
226.	Coffee (parchment), Groves Estate . . .	C. R. Taylor.
227.	Coffee (in cherry), Groves Estate	C. R. Taylor.
228.	Coffee (No. 1), Rose Hill Estate	Rev. J. Seed Roberts.
229.	Coffee (No. 2), Rose Hill Estate	Rev. J. Seed Roberts.
230.	Coffee (No. 3), Rose Hill Estate	Rev. J. Seed Roberts.
231.	Coffee (peaberry), Rose Hill Estate . . .	Rev. J. Seed Roberts.
232.	Coffee (in cherry), Rose Hill Estate . . .	Rev. J. Seed Roberts.
233.	Coffee (in parchment), Rose Hill Estate . .	Rev. J. Seed Roberts.
234.	Coffee (No. 1), Prospect Estate	Rev. J. Seed Roberts.
235.	Coffee (No. 2), Prospect Estate	Rev. J. Seed Roberts.
236.	Coffee (No. 3), Prospect Estate	Rev. J. Seed Roberts.
237.	Coffee (No. 1 of 1884-85 crop), Prospect Estate .	Rev. J. Seed Roberts.
238.	Coffee (peaberry), Prospect Estate . . .	Rev. J. Seed Roberts.
239.	Coffee (in cherry), Prospect Estate . . .	Rev. J. Seed Roberts.
240.	Coffee, Mount Cressy Estate	P. Desnoes & Son.
241.	Coffee, Park Hall Estate	H. J. Ronaldson.
242.	Coffee (peaberry), Park Hall Estate . . .	H. J. Ronaldson.
243.	Coffee, Sherwood Forest Estate	R. A. Stewart.
244.	Coffee, Sherwood Forest Estate	R. A. Stewart.
245.	Coffee (peaberry), Sherwood Forest Estate .	R. A. Stewart.
246.	Coffee (Mocha), Rose Hill Estate	Rev. J. Seed Roberts.
247.	Coffee (Liberian), Hordley Estate . . .	J. Harrison.
248.	Coffee (settlers), Golden Spring Estate . .	W. C. Logan.
249.	Coffee (settlers), Whitney Estate	George Wilson.
250.	Coffee (settlers), Whitney Estate	George Wilson.
251.	Coffee (settlers), Langley Estate	W. E. Sant.
252.	Coffee (settlers in parchment), Langley Estate .	W. E. Sant.
253.	Coffee (settlers)	Walter Logan.
254.	Coffee (settlers)	Walter Logan.

255. Coffee (settlers)	.	.	.	George & Branday.
256. Coffee (settlers)	.	.	.	George & Branday.
257. Coffee (cherries in solution).				Botanical Department.
258. Coffee (Liberian) .	.	.		Botanical Department.

VII.—PIMENTO.

Jamaica pepper or allspice, the dried and cured berries of a native tree (Pimenta vulgaris), was exported to the value of £53,867 in 1885. Jamaica supplies the world with this article, which is exported in large quantities from no other country. The pimento tree, which is allied to the myrtle family, grows abundantly on warm limestone hills at elevations of from 1,500 to 2,500 feet. Beneath the trees cattle and horses are pastured, feeding on the nutritious "pimento grass."

259.	Pimento, Bamboo Penn, Beresford Estate	.	.	S. Gossett.
260.	Pimento, Southfield Estate .	.	.	Richard Moss.
261.	Pimento, Lillyfield Estate .	.	.	Richard Moss.
262.	Pimento, Belle Vue Estate .	.	.	John Davidson.
263.	Pimento, Liberty Hill Estate	.	.	Miss Stennett.
264.	Pimento, Whitney Estate .	.	.	E. C. Elliott.
265.	Pimento, Seville Estate	.	.	J. E. P. Thompson.
266.	Pimento, Oldsbury Estate .	.	.	W. Pierce.
267.	Pimento, Middleton Estate .	.	.	George Massey.
268.	Pimento . . .	.	.	C. M. Calder.
269.	Pimento . . .	.	.	J. P. Baillie.
270.	Pimento . . .	.	.	E. S. Falden.
271.	Pimento . . .	.	.	George & Branday.
272.	Pimento . . .	.	.	George & Branday.
273.	Pimento . . .	.	.	T. G. Anthony.

VIII.—CACAO.

Cacao, or chocolate, is made from the cured beans or seeds of a tree (Theobroma Cacao). In connection with the development of the fruit trade in Jamaica, cacao is receiving great attention, and plantations are being established under the shade of the banana trees. To yield fine cacao, the beans require to be fermented and carefully cured. On the manner with which these processes are performed depend entirely the quality of the cacao. During the last three years, owing to better preparation, the price of Jamaica cacao has risen about 10 per cent. ; and, if systematic attention is paid to the curing of this article, planters may expect a considerable increase on the present market value. Many years ago Long, the historian, made the following remarks with regard to cacao: "This tree once grew so plentifully in Jamaica that the inhabitants flattered themselves it would become the source of inexhaustible wealth to them ; in 1671 there were forty-five walks in bearing, and many new ones in cultivation, but some years afterwards they were all destroyed at once, as it is said, by a blast which pervaded the whole island ; so that they were never afterwards recovered, and at present there are but few." The number of cacao plantations at present is about ten, but several smaller ones are being established, and it is hoped shortly to find Jamaica cacao in the London market in large quantities.

274. Cacao, Belle Vue Estate . . . . . John Davidson.
275. Cacao, Alpha Cottage Estate . . . . W. S. Taylor.
276. Cacao (washed and clayed), Golden Spring Estate W. Logan.
277. Cacao (fermented and washed), Golden Spring Estate . . . . W. Logan.
278. Cacao (fermented and washed), Langley Estate . W. E. Sant.
279. Cacao, Cambrian Plantation Estate . . . J. Cohen.
280. Cacao (No. 1), Spring Hill Estate . . . Rev. J. Seed Roberts.
280a. Cacao (No. 2), Spring Hill Estate . . . Rev. J. Seed Roberts.
281. Cacao (No. 3), Spring Hill Estate . . . Rev. J. Seed Roberts.
282. Cacao, Spring Hill Estate . . . . . Rev. J. Seed Roberts.
283. Cacao, Spring Hill Estate . . . . . Rev. J. Seed Roberts.
284. Cacao, Spring Hill Estate . . . . . Rev. J. Seed Roberts.
285. Cacao . . . . George & Branday.
286. Cacao (settlers), St. Thomas-in-the-Vale Estate . W. Logan.
287. Cacao (pods in spirit) . . . . . . Rev. J. Seed Roberts.
288. Cacao (leaves) . . . . Rev. J. Seed Roberts.
289. Cacao (butter) . . . . G. Eustace Burke.

IX.—ANNATTO.

Annatto is derived from the seeds of *Bixa Orellana*, a low shrubby tree, native of the West Indies. The seeds are prepared by drying in the sun, and when cured present a waxy, reddish colour. They are much used for colouring purposes.

290. Annatto, The Cottage Estate . . . . A. W. Kemble.
291. Annatto, Kingston Estate . . . . . H. Priest.
292. Annatto, Kingston Estate . . . . . A. S. Lazarus & Co.
293. Annatto, Kingston Estate . . . . . P. Desnoes & Son.
294. ʹAnnatto . . . . J. P. Baillie.
295. Annatto, precipitate from seeds without aid of chemicals, Union Hill Estate . . . . F. B. Sturridge.
296. Annatto, cleaned seeds, Union Hill Estate . . F. B. Sturridge.
297. Annatto, seeds in natural state, Union Hill Estate F. B. Sturridge.
298. Annatto and lard, free from foreign substance, slightly salted, Union Hill Estate . . . F. B. Sturridge.
299. Annatto, washings, after principal colouring matter has been extracted—showing colouring portion of seeds which is soluble in water, Union Hill Estate . . . . . F. B. Sturridge.
300. Annatto seed and olive oil, free from foreign substance, Union Hill Estate . . . . F. B. Sturridge.
301. Annatto and petroleum, fancy mixture, showing amalgamation of colouring matter with any oleaginous substances, Union Hill . . . F. B. Sturridge.

302.	Annatto, Worthy Park Estate	J. Gray.
303.	Colours from annatto precipitate, painted on paper, Union Hill Estate	F. B. Sturridge.
304.	Plate painted with annatto and paint oil, Union Hill Estate	F. B. Sturridge.
305.	Plate painted with annatto and olive oil, Union Hill Estate	F. B. Sturridge.

X.—FANCY AND FURNITURE WOODS.

It may be mentioned that there are no large forests in Jamaica from whence quantities of cheap building timber can be obtained. There are, however, choice cabinet and fancy woods which might be obtained in appreciable quantities, and the immense variety of articles such as knife-handles, knobs, buttons, &c., which are now manufactured from choice grained woods, opens a ready market to some of the best and most costly of Jamaica woods. Many of these woods, as may be seen at the Indian and Colonial Exhibition, are of surpassing excellence. Full particulars respecting the quantity obtainable, and the prices, may be had on application to the private exhibitors mentioned below.

(A.)—Woods in Polished Sections with Natural Bark.

306.	Lignum vitæ, Guaiacum officinale . . .	Botanical Department.
307.	Candle wood, Cassia emarginata . . .	Botanical Department.
308.	Yellow sanders (two), Bucida capitata . .	Botanical Department.
309.	Log wood (two), Hæmatoxylon campechianum .	Botanical Department.
310.	Log wood, Hæmatoxylon campechianum . .	Botanical Department.
311.	Fustic, Muclura tinctoria	Botanical Department.
312.	Bitter wood, Picræna excelsa	Botanical Department.
313.	Cam wood. Baphia nitida	Botanical Department.
314.	Prickly yellow, Xanthoxylon clava-Herculis .	Botanical Department.
315.	Calabash, Crescentia Cujete	Botanical Department.
316.	Cocoanut, Cocos nucifera	Botanical Department.
317.	Camphor wood (two), Cinnamomum camphora	Botanical Department.
318.	Cork wood (three), Anona palustris . . .	Botanical Department.
319.	Ebony, Brya Ebenus	Botanical Department.
320.	Wild Cinnamon, Canella alba	Botanical Department.
321.	Scarlet Cordia, Cordia Sebestena . . .	Botanical Department.
322.	Hog gum (two), Moronobea coccinea . .	Botanical Department.
323.	Quassia wood, Quassia amara	Botanical Department.
324.	Beech, Exostemma caribbæa	Botanical Department.
325.	Red bull heart	Botanical Department.
326.	Guava, Sidium Guava	Botanical Department.
327.	Fiddle wood, Catharexylum surrectum . .	Botanical Department.
328.	Cashaw, Prosopis juliflora	Botanical Department.
329.	Yoke, Catalpa longisiliqua	Botanical Department.
330.	Ginep, Melicocca bijuga	Botanical Department.
331.	Iron wood	Botanical Department.
332.	Red musk wood	S. T. Scharschmidt.
333.	Pimento	George & Branday.
334.	Lignum vitæ	George & Branday.

(B.)—Woods in Polished Slabs.

Exhibited by C. W. Trebarren, Bogue Estate, St. Elizabeth.

335. Green-heart ebony.
336. Fustic.
337. Naseberry bully tree.
338. Galimenta.
339. Wild tamarind.
340. Dog wood.
341. Pigeon wood.
342. Maiden plum.
343. Rose wood.
344. Yellow sanders.
345. Wild orange.
346. Bed wood.
347. Wild mahogany.
348. Pimento.
349. Fiddle wood.

351. Grape wood.
350. Log wood.
352. Yellow candle wood.
353. Black-heart ebony.
354. Bully tree.
355. Mammee bully tree.
356. Mahogany.
357. Brazilewood.
358. Cassada.
359. White candle wood.
360. Mahoe.
361. Bastard bully tree.
362. Bread nut.
363. Cog wood.

Exhibited by Turnbull & Madon, Kingston.

364. Mahogany.
365. Yacca.
366. Mahoe.
367. Satin wood.
368. Grey sanders.
369. Maiden plum.

370. Yoke.
371. Lace bark.
372. Dog wood.
373. Brazilewood.
374. Mahogany root.
375. Common cedar.

Exhibited by A. A. Green, Balaclava.

376. Mahogany.
377. Ebony.
378. Mahogany root.
379. Rose wood.
380. Red candle wood.
381. Bed bullet tree.
382. Fustic.
383. Bread nut.

384. Fiddle wood.
385. Cog bully tree.
386. Mahogany root.
387. White candle wood.
388. Blue mahoe.
389. Beech.
390. Green heart.

(C.)—Woods in Trimmed and Polished Blocks.

Exhibited by Alfred Pawsey, Kingston.

391. Mountain fig.
392. Prickly yellow.
393. Locust.
394. White dog wood.
395. White bullet wood.
396. Prune.

397. Timber sweet wood.
398. Grey sanders.
399. Broad leaf.
400. Dog wood.
401. Brazilewood.
402. Bread nut.

Exhibited by the Boys' Reformatory, Stony Hill.

403. Fiddle wood.
404. Mahogany.
405. Mahoe.
406. Black-heart ebony.
407. Yacca.
408. Prickly yellow.
409. Cocoanut.

410. Wild orange.
411. Spanish elm.
412. Satin wood.
413. Calabash.
414. Juniper cedar.
415. Pimento.
416. Yellow sanders.

(D.)—Woods in Small Polished Slabs, from the Parish of Clarendon.

Exhibited by Ernest C. Elliott, Vere.

417. Ants wood.
418. Beef apple.
419. Birch.
420. Braziletto, m.
421. Black bully tree.
422. Broad leaf.
423. Naseberry bully tree.
424. Bullet tree, l.
425. Wild bitter wood.
426. Barbary bully tree.
427. Break axe, m.
428. Bread nut, m.
429. Bread nut, l.
430. Bitter wood.
431. Blood wood.
432. Braziletto, m.
433. Beech.
434. Black ashes.
435. Braziletto, l.
436. Box wood, l.
437. Big family, l.
438. Cog wood.
439. Cedar.
440. Bastard cedar.
441. Calabash, m.
442. Calabash, l.
443. Red candle wood.
444. Wild candle wood.
445. White candle wood.
446. Cherry tree.
447. White cog wood.
448. Darrant cedar.
449. Cubla nancy.
450. Wild cinnamon.
451. Candle wood, l.
452. Cashaw, l.
453. Chink wood.
454. Damson.
455. Dog wood, m.
456. Dago.
457. Dog wood, l.
458. Black ebony, l.
459. Green-heart ebony, l.
460. Wild fiddle wood.
461. Wild fustic.
462. Fiddle wood.
463. Fustic.
464. Black fig.
465. Galimenta.
466. Gutter wood.
467. Wild guava.
468. Grand gini.

469. Wild ginep.
470. Grape, m.
471. Guava, l.
472. Guava, m.
473. Gum wood.
474. Tame guava.
475. Small-leaf grape.
476. Broad-leaf grape.
477. Green heart, l.
478. Mountain guava.
479. Hog doctor.
480. Wild hog doctor.
481. Iron wood, l.
482. White iron wood.
483. Jack fruit, l.
484. Jointer.
485. Lablab.
486. Lance wood.
487. Log wood, m.
488. Log wood, l.
489. Log wood root, l.
490. White lance wood.
491. Wild locust.
492. Bastard lignum vitæ.
493. Bastard lignum vitæ, l.
494. Mahogany.
495. Mountain ebony.
496. Milk wood.
497. Wild mahoe.
498. White mahogany.
499. Maiden plum.
500. Mango.
501. Mammee.
502. Mammee, sapote.
503. Wild mahogany.
504. Maroon lance.
505. Muskmelon.
506. Mast wood.
507. Mountain mahoe.
508. Wild orange.
509. Seville orange.
510. Wild olive, l.
511. Wild pomegranate.
512. Prune.
513. Prickly yellow.
513½. Parrot wood.
514. Pasture wood.
515. Pimento wood.
516. Pear tree.
517. Pepper wood.
518. Wild pear tree.
519. Prickly yellow, l.

520.	Prickly yellow root, l.	537.	Salt wood.
521.	Red rod wood.	538.	Satin wood.
522.	White rod wood.	539.	Wild Spanish olive.
523.	Rose wood.	540.	Stock fish, l.
524.	Rose apple.	541.	Small leaf, l.
525.	Rosin.	542.	White tamarind.
526.	Wild sour sop.	543.	Red tamarind.
527.	Spanish elm.	544.	Bastard tamarind.
528.	Wild Spanish elm.	545.	Turkey berry.
529.	Pepper sweet wood.	546.	Thatch wood.
530.	Belly sweet wood.	547.	Vanilla.
531.	Timber sweet wood.	548.	Wattle wood.
532.	Long-leaved sweet wood.	549.	Yellow sanders, l.
533.	Savannah barlary.	550.	Yellow sanders, m.
534.	Slug wood.	551.	Yoke wood.
535.	Slug sweet wood.	552.	Yacca.
536.	Silver wood.		

"l" signifies woods indigenous to the lowlands, " m " to the mountains.

XI.—SPICES, CONDIMENTS, &c.

Next to the development of the fruit interest, the cultivation of spices and spice plants would appear to offer great inducements in Jamaica. Pimento, which is the largest spice industry in the world, stands essentially a Jamaican product. Jamaica ginger is exported to the value of £20,000 per annum. Cayenne pepper, turmeric root, nutmeg, cinnamon, cardamom clove, vanilla, and black pepper are also established in the island, and afford abundant means for the prosecution of the minor industries. All the above-mentioned plants are chiefly cultivated in the low country.

559.	Cayenne pepper	Governors of Jamaica Institute.
560.	Cayenne pepper	B. Fisher.
561.	Cayenne pepper	B. Fisher.
562.	Cayenne pepper	Mrs. J. Bruce.
563.	Ginger	George & Branday.
564.	Ginger	P. Desnoes & Son.
565.	Ginger	George & Branday.
566.	Nutmegs, Bath	Dr. Major.
567.	Nutmegs, with mace, Bath . . .	Dr. Major.
568.	Nutmegs, in shell, Bath	Dr. Major.
569.	Nutmegs, out of shell, Bath . . .	Dr. Major.
570.	Nutmegs (in solution) . . .	Botanical Department.
571.	Turmeric powder	Botanical Department.
572.	Cinnamon	Botanical Department.
573.	Cinnamomum Cassia	Botanical Department.
574.	Wild cinnamon (Canella alba) . . .	Botanical Department.
575.	Cardamoms, Langley	W. E. Sant.
576.	Jamaica pickles, Kingston . . .	Levien & Sherlock.

XII.—MEALS, STARCHES.

Plants for the production of meals and starches are abundant in Jamaica, and they are capable of being produced in large quantities.

577.	Affoo Yam Meal, Whitney Estate	E. C. Elliott.
578.	Cocoa Meal, Whitney Estate	E. C. Elliott.
579.	Breadfruit meal, Whitney Estate	E. C. Elliott.
580.	Pumpkin meal, Whitney Estate	E. C. Elliott.
581.	Sweet potato starch, Gordon Town	J. Hart.
582.	Arrowroot starch, Worthy Park	J. Gray.
583.	Indian arrowroot starch, Worthy Park	J. Gray.
584.	Negro Yam starch, Whitney Estate	E. C. Elliott.
585.	Arrowroot starch, Plantain Garden River	Robert Kirkland.
586.	Cassava starch, Whitney Estate	E. C. Elliott.
587.	Starch, Whitney Estate	E. C. Elliott.
588.	Arrowroot starch	Governor's Jamaica Institute.
589.	Curcuma starch	Botanical Department.
590.	Tous les mois, Worthy Park	J. Gray.
591.	Sugar bean	Governor's Institute of Jamaica.
592.	White pea	Governor's Institute of Jamaica.
593.	No eye pea	Governor's Institute of Jamaica.
594.	Red pea	Governor's Institute of Jamaica.
595.	Cuckhold's Increase	Governor's Institute of Jamaica.
596.	Crab eye	Governor's Institute of Jamaica.

XIII.—DYEWOODS.

Dyewoods, such as log wood, fustic and sappan wood, are exported from Jamaica to the value of about £100,000 annually. Log wood was introduced from British Honduras in 1715, and since that time has spread spontaneously over the lowlands, especially in the neighbourhood of sugar estates, so that now the exports of log wood from Jamaica exceed those of British Honduras.

597.	Logwood, Elim Estate.	J. M. Farquharson.
598.	Fustic, Elim Estate	J. M. Farquharson.
599.	Sappan, Elim Estate	J. M. Farquharson.

XIV.—FIBRES AND FIBROUS MATERIALS.

Numerous plants are found in Jamaica capable of yielding valuable fibre, and considerable interest is being taken in the result of systematic trials undertaken by a committee appointed by government, to test the capabilities of certain machines driven by steam power in the preparation of fibres on a commercial scale. Experiments have been carried on during the last few years, beginning with a machine invented by a local engineer, Mr. James Kennedy, called the "Eureka" machine, and continued with a machine known as "Smith's Patent," manufactured by Death and Ellwood, Leicester, England, now the property of the Universal Fibre Company, London. The result of these trials have been published in the *Jamaica Gazette*, and, although not quite so satisfactory as was expected, still point to the fact that a fibre industry in Jamaica carried on in a systematic manner must prove highly remunerative.

Should a fibre industry be established in Jamaica, it will be necessary to cultivate the plants on a large scale. Many of these plants, such as the silk grass or henequen (*Furcræa cubensis*), the bowstring hemps (*Sansevieria*), and the China grass or Ramie (*Bœhmeria nivea*), are sufficiently abundant to supply plants to establish large areas at once.

(A.)—Specimens of Fibre Exhibited by Mr.James Kennedy, Kingston, Prepared by the "Eureka" Fibre Machine.

600. One bundle of fibres of pine-apple, Ramie, Pita.
601. Furcræa and Sansevieria zeylanica.
602. Bowstring hemp (Sansevieria zeylanica).
603. African bowstring hemp (Sansevieria guineensis).
604. Ramie (Bœhmeria nivea).
605. Plantain (Musa paradisiaca).
606. Dagger (Yucca aloifolia).
607. Pinguin (Bromelia pinguin).
608. Flag or rush (Cladium occidentale).
609. Pine-apple (Ananas sativa).
610. Keratto (Agave keratto).
611. Bromelia Karatas.

(B.)—Exhibited by the Governor's Institute of Jamaica.

612. Silk grass (Furcræa cubensis).
613. Pinguin (Bromelia pinguin).
614. Keratto cleaned and extracted (Agave keratto).
615. Pine-apple (Ananas sativa).
616. Bowstring hemp (Sansevieria zeylanica).
617. African bowstring hemp (Sansevieria guineensis).
618. Dagger, cleaned (Yucca aloifolia).
619. Ramie (Bœhmeria nivea).

XV.—OILS, ESSENTIAL OIL, PERFUMES, &c.

Plants yielding oils and perfumes are abundant in Jamaica, and exhibits enumerated below indicate a wide field for the operations of the chemist and the cultivator of flowers for their perfumes. Many of the plants are very abundant and obtainable in large quantities; others, like the tube rose and jasmine, require to be cultivated. The first attempt to establish a flower-farm and extract perfume in the island is being made by Col. Talbot, on Worthy Park Estate, St. Catherine (under the superintendence of Mr. J. Gray).

(A.)—Exhibited by S. T. Scharschmidt, Mandeville.

620. Tuberose pomade (Polianthes tuberosa).
621. Jasmine pomade (Jasminum sp.).
622. Extracts of Bonplondia.
623. Extract of wild cinnamon (Canella alba).
624. Extract of vanilla (Vanilla planifolia).
625. Extract of jasmine and Lily.
626. Extract of jasmine (Jasminum sp.).
627. Extract of red muskwood.
628. Extract of rosewood.
629. Extract of Tangierine orange (Citrus Aurantium var.).
630. Extract of verbena.
631. Essential oil of lemon (Citrus medica var. Limonum).
632. Essential oil of sweet orange (Citrus Aurantium).
633. Essential oil of Seville orange (Citrus Aurantium).
634. Essential oil of pimento berries (Pimenta vulgaris).
635. Essential oil of pimento leaf (Pimenta vulgaris).
636. Fixed oil of Ben nut.
637. Fixed oil of pear (Persea gratissima).
638. Fixed oil of walnut (Aleurites triloba).

(B.)

639. Walnut oil (Aleurites triloba), Ocho Rios, A. J. Rodgers.
640. Essential oil, Seville orange (Citrus Aurantium var.), Worthy Park, J. Gray.
641. Essential oil, sweet orange (Citrus Aurantium), Worthy Park, J. Gray.
642. Essential oil of citron lime, Worthy Park, J. Gray.

(C.)—Exhibited by J. J. Bowrey, F.C.S., F.I.C., Government Analytical Chemist.

643. Essential oil, Mountain cigar bush (Hedyosmum nutans).
644. Essential oil, Blue gum (Eucalyptus Globulus).
645. Essential oil, Seville orange seed (Citrus Aurantium var.).
646. Essential oil, Cigar bush (Critonia Dalea).
647. Essential oil, Lemon grass (Andropogon citratus).
648. Essential oil, Juniper cedar (Juniperus bermudiana).
649. Essential oil, Mountain thyme (Micromeria obovata).
650. Essential oil, Pimento leaves (Pimenta vulgaris).
651. Essential oil of Ben (Moringa pterygosperma).
652. Essential oil of Cocoanut (Cocos nucifera).
653. Essential oil, Spanish walnut (Aleurites triloba).
654. Essential oil, Sand box (Hura crepitans).
655. Essential oil, Santa Maria (Calophyllum calaba).
656. Essential oil, matter of Annotta (Bixa orellana).
657. Fat of Antidote Cacoon (Fevillea cordifolia).

XVI.—MEDICINAL AND ECONOMIC SUBSTANCES.

Plants of a medicinal nature are a marked feature in the indigenous Flora of Jamaica, and in works published from 1735 to the present time numerous references are made to the valuable properties possessed by Jamaica plants. Cinchona (150 acres) and Tea (2 acres) are cultivated experimentally by Government. The following exhibit contains a fairly representative collection of the medicinal plants (both indigenous and introduced) of the island. The reference in brackets indicates the portion of the plant used in medicine :—

(A.)—Exhibits by the Botanical Department, Jamaica.

658. Nickar seeds, Guilandina Bonducella.
659. Nickar seeds, Guilandina Bonduc.
660. Nickar seeds, Guilandina Bonduc. var.
661. Horse-eye beans, Mucuna urens.
662. Horse beans.
663. Wild worm wood (leaves), Parthenium hysterophorus.
664. Pepper rod (leaves), Croton humilis.
665. Guinea hen weed (whole plant), Petiveria alliacea.
666. Sand box seeds, Hura crepitans.
667. Castor oil seed, Ricinus communis.
668. Guaco (root and leaves), Mikania guaco.
669. Bottle-cod root, Capparis cyanophallophora.
670. Adrue (tubers), Cyperus articulatus.
671. Pomegranate (rind of fruit), Punica granatum.
672. Dog wood (bark), Piscida erythrina.
673. Locust tree bark, Hymenæa courbaril.
674. Bastard cabbage bark, Andira inermis.
675. Balsam tree bark, Amyris balsamifera.
676. China root, Smilax China.
677. Fitweed root, Eryngium fœtidum.
678. False ipecacuanha, Asclepias curassavica.
679. Cow-itch (pods), Mucuna urens.
680. Divi-divi pods, Cæsalpinia coriaria.
681. Surge weed, Euphorbia pilulifera.
682. Horse cassia, Cassia fistula.
683. Mexican thistle seed, Argemone mexicana.
684. Cascarilla bark, Croton cascarilla.
685. Locust tree gum, Hymenæa courbaril.
686. Gum guaiacum, Guaiacum officinale.
687. Log wood gum, Hæmatoxylon campechinum.
688. Horse cassia, Cassia grandis.
689. Purging cassia, Cassia fistula.
690. Crabs-eye or jequetery seeds, Abrus precatorius.
691. Circassian beads, Adenanthera pavonina.
692. Soap berry, Sapindus inæqualis.
693. Job's tears, Coix lachryma.
694. Maiden plum bark, Comocladia integrifolia
695. Wild cinnamon bark, Canella alba.
696. John Crow bush (roots), Bocconia frutescens.
697. Prune bark, Prunus occidentalis.
698. Mountain Cigar bush (leaves), Hedyosmum nutans.
699. Bitter Dan bark, Simaruba glauca.
700. Blue gum trees (leaves), Eucalyptus globulus.
701. Lemon-scented gum tree, Eucalyptus citriodora.
702. Antidote cacoon, Fevillea cordifolia.
703. French Cotton, Calotropis procera.
704. Cacoon seeds, Entada scandens.
705. Hog gum, Moronobea coccinea.

706. Maté or Paraquay Tea, Ilex paraguayensis.
707. African oil palm seeds, Elæis guineensis.
708. Ccará rubber seed, Manihot glaziovi.
709. Jamaica walnut, Aleurites triloba.
710. Para rubber seeds, Hevea braziliensis.
711. Betel nut seeds, Areca catechu.
712. Kus-kus grass (root), Andropogon muricatus.
713. Chewstick (branches), Gouania domingensis.
714. Cotton.
715. Sarsaparilla (roots), Smilax officinalis.
716. Mahogany seed, Swietenia mahagoni.
717. Breadfruit tree (leaves), Artocarpus incisa.
718. African sweet reed (5 vars.), Sorghum spp.
719. Aloes (inspissated juice), Aloe vulgaris.

(B.)—Contributed by Private Parties.

720. Jamaica walnut (Aleurites triloba) . . . . Dr. Major.
721. Kola nut (Cola acuminata) . . . . . Dr. Major.
722. Locust tree gum (Hymenæa courbaril) . . . Mrs. T. Hendrick.
723. Cashew gum (Anacardium occidentale) . . . Mrs. T. Hendrick.
724. Hog gum (Moronobea coccinea) . . . . Rev. J. Seed Robert
725. Kola nut (Cola acuminata) . . . . . Rev. J. Seed Roberts.
726. Kus-kus grass (root), (Andropogon muricatus) . J. Gray.
727. Coca leaves, No. 1 (Erythroxylon coca) . . . Rev. J. Seed Roberts.
728. Coca leaves, No. 2 (Erythroxylon coca) . . . Rev. J. Seed Roberts.
729. Liquorice seed . . . . Miss L. Gordon.
730. Divi-divi pods (Cæsalpinia coriaria) . . . John Thompson.
731. Cashaw gum (Prosopis juliflora) . . . . S. T. Scharschmidt.
732. Cashaw gum (Anacardium occidentale) . . . S. T. Scharschmidt.
733. Log wood gum (Hæmatoxylon campechianum) . S. T. Scharschmidt.
734. Locust tree gum (Hymenæa courbaril) . . . S. T. Scharschmidt.
735. Cascarilla bark (Croton cascarilla) . . . . S. T. Scharschmidt.
736. Wild cinnamon bark (Canella alba) . . . . S. T. Scharschmidt.
737. Sarsaparilla (Smilax officinalis) . . . . A. Berry.
738. Soap berries (Sapindus inæqualis) . . . . Rev. E. Palmer.
739. St. Vincent seeds . . . . Rev. E. Palmer.
740. Rice (grown in Clarendon) . . . . . Rev. E. Palmer.
741. Syrup made from horehound, liquorice, &c. . . Miss Rebecca Martin.

(C.)—Prepared by J. J. Bowrey, F.I.C., F.C.S., Government Analytical Chemist.

742. Cinchona febrifuge, prepared from Jamaica-grown bark of Cinchona succirubra.

XVII.—MISCELLANEOUS.

(A.)

743. Honey, Kingston . . . . P. Desnoes & Son.
744. Honey, St. Catherine . . . . . . Matthew Russell.
745. Honey, Kingston . . . . J. H. Aikman.
746. Honey, St. Catherine . . . . . . Charles Gordon.
747. Beeswax (bleached), St. Catherine . . . . Matthew Russell.

748.	Beeswax, Kingston	.	.	.	.	A. Berry.
749.	Beeswax, St. Catherine	.	.	.	.	Charles Gordon.
750.	Beeswax, Kingston	.	.	.	.	George & Branday.
751.	Lime juice, Black River	.	.	.	.	George E. Levy.
752.	Lime juice, Lillyfield	.	.	.	.	Richard Moss.
753.	Preserved Ginger	.	.	.	.	Arthur Linton.
754.	Lime juice, Southfield	.	.	.	.	Richard Moss.
755.	Vinegar	.	.	.	.	James Verley.
756.	Citrate of lime, Mandeville	.	.	.	.	S. T. Scharschmidt.
757.	Buckets of common bamboo (Bambusa vulgaris)	.				Botanical Department.
758.	Yams	.	.	.	.	Governor's Institute of Jamaica.
759.	African yam	.	.	.	.	D. Morris.
760.	Arracacha (Arracacha esculenta)	.	.	.		Botanical Department
761.	Old man's beard (Tillandsia usneoides)	.	.			Botanical Department.
762.	Assam tea, prepared from plants growing on the Government Cinchona Plantation, Jamaica	.				J. Hart.

(B.)—Exhibited by Levien & Sherlock, Kingston.

763. A turtle back.
764. Turtle tablets for epicures.
765. Turtle tablets for invalids.
766. Turtle fat.
767. Eggs from interior of a turtle.
768. Turtle eggs found in the sand.
769. Turtle diamonds.
770. Turtle oil.
771. Dry turtle.
772. Preserves in bottles, of ginger, limes, orange, cherimoya, melon, cashaw, pine-apple, No. 11 mango, green tamarinds, crystallised ginger, guava jelly, mangolima.
773. Preserves of Jamaica fruits in tins.

(C.)—Exhibited by the General Penitentiary.

774. Tubs.
775. Piggins.
776. A chess table of Jamaica woods.
777. A pair of boots.
778. A staff.
779. Rulers.
780. A what-not.
781. Hats.

XVIII.—BOOKS, REPORTS, &c.

782. Set of volumes of the "Handbook of Jamaica" for the years 1882, 1883, 1884-85, 1885-86, compiled by A. C. Sinclair and L. R. Fyfe.
783. Set of volumes of the "Handbook of Jamaica" for the years 1882, 1833, 1884-85, 1885-86, exhibited by the Governors of the Institute of Jamaica.
784. Studies on the Flora of Jamaica, Mrs. T. Hendrick.
785. Map of the Island of Jamaica by Governor's Institute of Jamaica.
786. Departmental Reports for the year 1883-84.
787. Jamaica Blue-Book for the year 1884.

XIX.—VIEWS, PHOTOGRAPHS, PLANS, AND BOTANICAL SPECIMENS, MOUNTED IN FRAMES.

(A.)—Contributed by the Governors of the Institute of Jamaica.

788. Craigton Church, Port Royal Mountains.
789. Irish Town, Port Royal Mountains.
790. Port Royal, Naval Station.
791. The Bog Walk, on Road to St. Ann's.
792. A view of the Town of Mandeville.
793. A view of the Town of Lucea.
794. Roaring River Bridge, St. Ann's.
795. The Cotton Tree, Up-Park Camp.
796. Old Queen's House, Spanish Town.
797. River Head.
798. View of a Village, Stewart Town.
799. A view of the Fern Walk.
800. Port Maria, North Coast.
801. A view of Harbour Street, Kingston.
802. Y. S. Falls.
803. Barracks of the 2nd West India Regiment, Up-Park Camp.
804. A view of Duke Street, Kingston.
805. Strawberry Hill, Mountain Residence.
806. Newcastle, Hill Station for White Troops.
807. Metcalf's Statue, Kingston.
808. A view of Newcastle.
809. Brooks's Hotel, Mandeville.
810. The Bog Walk.
811. View on the Road to Newcastle.
812. King's House, Governor's Residence, near Kingston.
813. A view on the Bog Walk.
814. Part of the Bog Walk.
815. Montego Bay.
816. Court House, Black River.
817. The Cocoanut Grove at the Lunatic Asylum, Kingston.
818. Cascade, Roaring River.
819. Viaduct on the Ewarton Extension Line.
820. The Bog Walk.
821. Cascade of the Roaring River.
822. Dam Head, Irrigation Works.
823. Hamstead Estate, Trelawny.
824. The Rio Cobre, Spanish Town.
825. Llandovery Falls, St. Ann's.
826. Band of the 1st West India Regiment.
827. The Dining Hall of the Lunatic Asylum, Kingston.
828. Male Recreation Court, Lunatic Asylum, Kingston.
829. Male and Female Dormitories, Lunatic Asylum, Kingston.
830. Male Infirmary, Lunatic Asylum, Kingston.
831. Gate Lodge, Hospital, &c., Lepers' Home, Spanish Town.
832. Ward and Recreation Shed, Male, Lepers' Home, Spanish Town.
833. Male Ward, Front View, Public Hospital, Kingston.
834. Male Ward, Side View, Public Hospital, Kingston.
835. Operation Theatre and Wards, Public Hospital, Kingston.

(B.)—Exhibited by the Rev. Barton Tucker, Port Royal.

836. View from a West India Verandah.
837. A Banana Tree.
838. Fort Augusta, &c.
839. Corner of a Provision Ground.
840. Garrison and Point, Port Royal.
841. Near Kingston, from Port Royal.
842. View in the Public Gardens.
843. View of the Interior of May Penn.
844. Up in the Hills.
845. Group of Bamboos, Chapelton.
846. Tavernor, Chapelton.
847. Cabbage Palm, &c.
848. Date Palm, &c.
849. Cocoanut Palm and Mangroves.
850. Up in the Hills.
851. St. Catherine's Peak.
852. Red Hills Village, under Bull Head.
853. In the Palisadoes.
854. In the Grounds, King's House.
855. Port Royal, from Craighton.
856. Kingston from the Palisadoes (framed oil painting).
857. "In the Isle of Springs" (framed oil painting).

(C.)

858. Newcastle, from Flamstead Road (oil painting), Col. Morley, Up-Park Camp.
859. Sunset at Harbour Head, Jamaica (oil painting), Mrs. Morley, Up-Park Camp.
860. Up-Park Camp (oil painting), Mrs. Morley, Up-Park Camp.
861. Up-Park Camp, showing Messhouse, Mrs. Morley, Up-Park Camp.
862. Photographs of the Parish Church, Kingston, Miss Downer.
863. A complete set of the postage stamps (from half-penny to five shillings) and of island and foreign post cards in use in Jamaica since 1860, contributed by the Postmaster for Jamaica.
864. A complete set of the telegraph stamps (three-pence and one shilling) and of the embossed stamps for general and Government use, issued in Jamaica, October 1879. Contributed by the Postmaster for Jamaica.
865. A set of revenue stamps and embossed stamps. Contributed by the Commissioner of Stamps, Jamaica.
866. Mounted specimen cards of Cinchona, Ferns, and Lichens, exhibited by the Botanical Department.

XX.—FANCY ARTICLES AND ORNAMENTAL WORK.

(A.)—From the Women's Self-Help Society, Kingston.

867. Two fire screens made from French cotton.
868. Two fire screens made from lace bark.
869. A birthday card.
870. A lamp shade.
871. A fan made from lace bark and ferns.
872. One set of d'oyleys.
873. A photograph screen made from dagger plant.
874. A letter rack made from dagger plant.
875. Necklaces made from "gold" shells.

876. Chains made of " Job's tears "
877. Chains made of "soap berries."
878. Chain made of shells.
879. Necklace made from liquorice seeds.
880. Watch pocket made from the "strainer" vine.
881. An etching on bamboo.
882. An etching on small bamboo.
883. A "Yabba."
884. A cocoanut, polished.
885. A small cocoanut, polished.
886. Handkerchief case made from banana bark.
887. Cigar case made from banana bark.
888. A pair of bracelets made from the horse-eye bean.
889. Napkin rings made from bamboo.
890. A basket made from leaves of the palmetto palm.
891. A hat made from leaves of the palmetto palm.
892. A " Tarantula " spider's nest.
893. Hat made of Jippijappa leaves.
894. Lace bark whip.
895. Specimen of lace bark.
896. Rings made from " gru-gru" nuts.
897. Scarf ring made from " gru-gru " nut.
898. Chains made from Circassian seeds.
899. Zulu hat basket covered with moss.
900. A pair of tortoise shell bracelets.
901. A pair of tortoise shell hair pins.
902. A set of tortoise shell studs, &c.
903. A pair of tortoise shell hair pins.
904. A picture made of lace bark, French cotton, &c.
905. Sticks from ebony and " gru-gru " palm.

(B.)—From Mrs. Hendrick, Richmond Park.

906. Water monkey of Jamaica pottery, with convolvulus, ferns, &c., painted in oils.
907. Flower pot, with flowering plantain painted in oils.
908. Flower pot, with Iris lily and coleus.
909. Two calabashes, with Jamaica flowers painted on them.
910. Two calabashes painted in blue.
911. One set of d'oyleys made from lace bark and Jamaica ferns.

(C.)—From Mrs. Morley, Up-Park Camp.

912. Twelve d'oyleys painted in oils.
913. Six d'oyleys painted in oils.
914. Twelve d'oyleys.
915. Cards ornamented with Jamaica ferns.
916. Bread-fruit blossoms.

(D.)—From Miss Downer, Kingston.

917. One set of d'oyleys made from lace bark and Jamaica ferns.
918. One lamp shade.
919. One set of candle shades.

(E.)—Exhibited by the Governors of the Institute of Jamaica.

920. Back combs made from tortoise shell.
921. Combs made from tortoise shell.

922. Dressing case comb from tortoise shell.
923. A pair of cuff bracelets of „ „
924. A pair of band bracelets of „ „
925. An amber bracelet of „ „
926. A chain made of „ „
927. A pocket comb of „ „
928. Paper knife of „ „
929. Brooch of „ „
930. Pair of ball amber earrings of „ „
931. Amber studs, &c., of „ „
932. Pins of „ „
933. Amber cross of „ „
934. Salt spoons of „ „

(F.)

935. Wall baskets of "Jippijappa," A. C. Bancroft, Buff Bay.
936. Fancy baskets, Miss M. R. Martin, Kingston.
937. Souvenir of Jamaica (in ferns), Mrs. Major, Bath.
938. Carved calabashes, Samuel Stephen.
939. Lamp shades, Miss Kilburn, Kingston.
940. A set of d'oyleys, Mrs. Hitchins, Kingston.
941. A dagger plant hat, Miss Egbertha Harrison, Ocho Rios.
942. Watch pockets from dagger plant, Miss Egbertha Harrison, Ocho Rios.
943. Pincushion from dagger plant, Miss Egbertha Harrison, Ocho Rios.
944. Fern albums, Miss Egbertha Harrison, Ocho Rios.
945. Hat made from wire grass, T. E. Thompson.
946. Ladies' basket made of wire grass, T. E. Thompson.
947. Dish-mats made of wire grass, T. E. Thompson.

XXI.—EXHIBITS of SALT from the TURKS and CAICOS ISLANDS, DEPENDENCIES OF JAMAICA, W. I.

948. Five barrels, J. W. Reynolds, Turks Island.
949. One box, Frith & Murphy, Turks Island.

XXII.—CINCHONA BARK.

FROM TREES GROWN IN THE BLUE MOUNTAINS OF JAMAICA.

(A.)—Exhibited by De B. S. Heaven, Whitfield Hall.

950. Trunk bark, Cinchona officinalis.
951. Twig bark, Cinchona officinalis.
952. Root bark, Cinchona officinalis.
953. Trunk bark, Cinchona succirubra.
954. Branch and twig bark, Cinchona succirubra.
955. Root bark, Cinchona succirubra.

(B.)—Exhibited by the Botanical Department.

956. Cinchona calisaya.
957. Cinchona hybrid.
958. Cinchona officinalis.
959. Cinchona Ledgeriana.
960. Cinchona succirubra.
961. Cinchona Ledgeriana (Howard's).

XXIII.—BAMBOOS, WALKING STICKS, &c.

The bamboo (*Bambusa vulgaris*) is generally distributed in Jamaica. In a crushed state it is exported for fibre and paper-making. Material for walking sticks is abundant. The wild cane (*Arundo occidentalis*) possesses roots of very grotesque shapes and forms which might be utilised for umbrella and sunshade handles. Of these roots large quantities are easily obtainable at a moderate cost.

Exhibited by the Botanical Department.

962. Stems of common bamboo (Bambusa vulgaris).
963. Stems of China bamboo (Bambusa nana).
964. Stems of solid bamboo (Bambusa sp.).
965. Stems of wild cane (Arundo occidentalis).
966. Stems of wild cane (Arundo saccharoides).
967. Stems of Indian cane (Beesha travancoriensis).
968. Stems of ground rattan (Rhaphis flabelliformis).

969. Walking Sticks, exhibited by the Governors of the Institute of Jamaica.

List of Articles collected in England
(in addition to the Exhibits from the Colony).

DYE WOODS.
Exhibited by Major J. Simpson-Carson.
Log wood in natural state.

MISCELLANEOUS.—BOTANICAL SPECIMENS, &c.
(A.)—Exhibited by Mrs. SIMPSON-CARSON.
Jamaica pressed ferns.
(B.)—Exhibited by Christy & Co.

Remijia Purdieana.
Mock pepper.
Papaw leaves.
Papaw dry juice.
Sarsaparilla.
Nutmeg and its fat.
Copalchi bark.
Blue Mountain coffee.
Black pepper seed.

Annatto seed (husk).
Jatropha Curcus.
Colubrina reclinata.
Euphorbia piluligera.
Capsicums.
Jamaica Chew-Stick.
Lucuma mammosa.
Guaiacum officinale.
Kola leaf.

Gum Guaiacum.
Cassia Sophera.
Parthenium hysterophorum.
Leucæna glauca.
Nutmegs.
Feuilla cordifolia.
Mucuna urens.

(C.)—Exhibited by C. Washington Eves.
GROWING PLANTS, VIZ.:—

Mahogany tree.
Dracæna.
Clusia.
India-rubber.
Cypress.
Musacoccinea.
Croupaum.
Lomaria gibba.

Aloe, variegated.
Coffea Arabica.
Lemon tree.
Alocasia edibilla (cocoa).
Orange tree.
Jamaica myrtle.
Blue gum.
Laurus canella.

Myristica fragrans.
Palm Latonia.
Musa.
Plantain.
Date palm.
Pandanus Vitchi.

FANCY ARTICLES.
(A.)—Exhibited by Miss Sewell.

Chains made of "Job's tears."
    „   „   liquorice seeds.
    „   „   St. Vincent seeds.

Chains made of soap-berries.
    „   „   nickle seeds.

(B.)—Exhibited by Hon. Henry Sewell.

Lamp-shades made from lace bark.
Lace bark whip.
D'oyleys made of lace bark.
Lace bark and Jamaica fans.
Seeds strung in necklaces.

Large alligator hide.
Large mounted alligator's head.
Specimen lace bark.
Sticks.

Exhibited by Hon. H. J. Kemble.
Oil of Ben.

Exhibited by Col. A. W. Chambers.
Fan and d'Oyleys made of lace bark and ferns.

PHOTOGRAPHS.
(A.)—Exhibited by Hon. R. H. JACKSON.

Pumbpoint Lighthouse, Port Royal, Jamaica.
Residence near Half-way Tree, St. Andrew's, Jamaica.
Arch erected at Half-way Tree, to welcome Sir Henry and Lady Norman on their return to Jamaica.
Half-way Tree Court House, Parish of St. Andrew's, Jamaica.
New Castle Station of English Troops in Jamaica.
Opening of Railroad from Kingston to the Moneague, by Sir Henry Norman.
Parish Church, Kingston, Jamaica.
Interior of Half-way Tree Court House, in the Parish of St. Andrew's, on the occasion of presentation of address to Sir Henry and Lady Norman.
Arrival of Sir Henry and Lady Norman on Royal Mail Steamer, at Kingston, Jamaica.
Public Gardens on the Parade, Kingston, Jamaica.
Arch of Welcome by the Kingston Volunteers to Sir Henry and Lady Norman.
Arch erected in Kingston to Welcome Sir Henry and Lady Norman on their return from England.

(B.)—Exhibited by Miss Norman.
Photograph of General Sir Henry Norman, K.C.B., &c., &c., Governor of Jamaica.

(C.)—Exhibited by C. Washington Eves.
Photograph of General Sir Henry Norman, K.C.B., &c., &c., Governor of Jamaica.
„ „ 1st West India Band, taken by the Stereoscopic Company, London.

LARGE OIL-PAINTINGS REPRESENTING JAMAICA SCENERY.
Exhibited by C. Washington Eves.
(Painted by H. P. Dollman and C. Washington Eves.)

Harbour Street, Kingston, 1825.
Montego Bay, 1810.
Kingston and Port Royal, 1805.
Bog Walk, 1820.
Port Maria.

Holland Estate, St. Thomas.
Steward's Bluff (sea view).
Green Island (sea view).
Coat-of-Arms (Jamaica).

SUNDRIES FROM JAMAICA.
Exhibited by C. Washington Eves.

Large alligator.
Small alligator.
Shark and flying-fish.
Six hammocks.
Two piles of rum casks, representing puncheons, hogsheads, barrels, quarter-casks, and octaves.
Case of humming-birds.
Two turtle-backs.
Carib implements.
Palm fans.
Pampas grass for decorative purposes.

SUGAR.
970. Exhibited by Major J. Simpson-Carson.
Albion vacuum pan (yellow)
971. Exhibited by C. Washington Eves.
Friendship Centrifugal (yellow).
972. Exhibited by Hawthorn, Sheddon, & Co.
Y. S. Estate Muscovado crop, 1886.

Exhibited by C. W. EVES & CO.

RUM.

No.		Mark		
973.	Carson	R H / A	Crop,	1885.
974.	„	A C	„	1886.
975.	Plummers'	F <> G	Crop,	1863.
976.	„	„	„	1864.
977.	„	„	„	1865.
978.	„	„	„	1866.
979.	„	„	„	1867.
980.	„	„	„	1868.
981.	„	„	„	1869.
982.	„	„	„	1870.
983.	„	„	„	1871.
984.	„	„	„	1872.
985.	„	„	„	1873.
986.	„	„	„	1874.
987.	„	„	„	1875.
988.	„	„	„	1876.
989.	„	„	„	1877.
990.	„	„	„	1878.
991.	„	„	„	1879.
992.	„	„	„	1880.
993.	„	„	„	1881.
994.	„	„	„	1882.
995.	Wedderburn's	P / I W	Crop,	1882.
996.	„	„	„	1885.
997.	Wedderburn's	R / I W	Crop,	1863.
998.	„	„	„	1864.
999.	„	„	„	1865.
1000.	„	„	„	1866.
1001.	„	„	„	1867.
1002.	„	„	„	1868.
1003.	„	„	„	1869.
1004.	„	„	„	1870.
1005.	„	„	„	1871.
1006.	„	„	„	1872.
1007.	„	„	„	1873.
1008.	„	„	„	1874.
1009.	„	„	„	1875.
1010.	„	„	„	1876.
1011.	„	„	„	1877.
1012.	„	„	„	1878.
1013.	„	„	„	1879.
1014.	„	„	„	1880.
1015.	„	„	„	1881.
1016.	„	„	„	1882.
1017.	„	„	„	1883.
1018.	„	„	„	1884.
1019.	„	„	„	1885.
1020.	„	„	„	1886.
1021.	Mark	A / H S	Crop,	1885.
1022.	„	B C / A D	„	1879.
1023.	„	B B / A D	„	1879.
1024.	„	C ♡ G	„	1876.
1025.	„	C ♡ E	„	1879.
1026.	„	C / W G	„	1880.
1027.	„	D / HN	„	1874.
1028.	„	E / H S	„	1872.
1029.	„	F / W	„	1875.
1030.	„	G / T G	„	1870.
1031.	„	A G P W	„	1867.
1032.	„	G V	„	1874.
1033.	„	G G / ‡ ‡	„	1872.
1034.	„	H / F C	„	1878.
1035.	„	HI / H S	„	1872.
1036.	„	S T	„	1882.
1037.	„	H I ◇ C	„	1879.
1038.	„	D / HH	„	1879.
1039.	„	H / W G	„	1880.
1040.	„	K / ‡ I	„	1872.
1041.	„	W V / L H	„	1880.
1042.	„	L P	„	1881.
1043.	„	L / C G	„	1878.
1044.	„	A / N G	„	1882.

No.		Mark		Crop
1045.	Mark	O E	Crop,	1883.
1046.	"	O V / H N	"	1883.
1047.	"	C	"	1878.
1048.	"	C / G R C	"	1879.
1049.	"	S / S T	"	1880.
1050.	"	S / R M	"	1876.
1051.	"	T / I I	"	1874.
1052.	"	V R	"	1885.
1053.	"	G / A A	"	1879.
1054.	"	D E	"	1879.
1055.	"	A / T C	"	1878.
1056.	"	H / ML	"	1876.
1057.	"	G ◇ P	"	1875.
1058.	"	E / L H	"	1875.
1059.	"	R / I S	"	1875.
1060.	"	L / C L	"	1875.
1061.	"	HDE	"	1875.
1062.	"	S / I E	"	1877.
1063.	"	C / C L	"	1877.
1064.	"	E / S G	"	1876.
1065.	"	L L / A D	"	1878.
1066.	"	G / I E	"	1878.
1067.	"	I T / N R	"	1875.
1068.	"	T	"	1874.
1069.	"	W / I A N / V	"	1879.
1070.	"	R / C W	"	1878.
1071.	"	D H	"	1871.
1072.	"	S / E T	"	1878.
1073.	"	R / O N W	"	1874.

No.		Mark		Crop
1074.	Mark	L / W W	Crop,	1874.
1075.	"	V / I B	"	1880.
1076.	"	HH / T B	"	1881.
1077.	"	D / B ◇ G	"	1879.
1078.	"	M / I M	"	1879.
1079.	"	R / I C / Y	"	1875.
1080.	"	D / O N	"	1880.
1081.	"	P H / E	"	1869.
1082.	"	S C / W D	"	1877.
1083.	"	S I / I M	"	1877.
1084.	"	V / I C	"	1875.
1085.	"	V / B P	"	1875.
1086.	"	G F / Q	"	1883.
1087.	"	C / W S	"	1885.
1088.	"	P / I W	"	1885.
1089.	"	E / P	"	1885.
1090.	"	P / T B	"	1882.
1091.	"	A	"	1878.
1092.	"	A 1	"	1878.
1093.	"	T E	"	1878.
1094.	"	P / R H	"	1872.
1095.	"	R / C H	"	1872.
1096.	"	S / G R H	"	1870.
1097.	"	B / W	"	1870.
1098.	"	◇H	"	1885.
1099.	"	L / A E	"	1865.
1100.	"	G / I I	"	1875.

No.		Mark	Crop	Year
1101.	Mark	G / I I	Crop,	1880.
1102.	„	L / W M	„	1880.
1103.	„	L H K	„	1866.
1104.	„	◇R	„	1881.
1105.	„	C / J W P / M	„	1880.
1106.	„	C H / I I	„	1879.
1107.	„	U H	„	1880.
1108.	„	W / K	„	1878.
1109.	„	A / J S W	„	1884.
1110.	„	H	„	1883.
1111.	„	C / W C	„	1880.
1112.	„	G G	„	1876.
1113.	„	◇C / W & N	„	1879.
1114.	„	H / C C	„	1880.
1115.	„	F R	„	1880.
1116.	„	P ◇ P	„	1878.
1117.	„	◇Q	„	1875.
1118.	„	◇R D	„	1882.
1119.	„	H C / S T	„	1877.
1120.	„	F / W H K	„	1884.
1121.	„	A / O C / M	„	1878.
1122.	„	S V	„	1880.
1123.	„	P / I W	„	1878.
1124.	„	Q ◇ P	„	1867.
1125.	„	P ◇ H I	„	1880.
1126.	„	ÆJ	„	1878.
1127.	Mark	S ♡	Crop,	1872.
1128.	„	I W O	„	1876.
1129.	„	W / B	„	1876.
1130.	„	I ◇ W	„	1879.
1131.	„	L^C	„	1873.
1132.	„	M G M	„	1873.
1133.	„	S ♡ F	„	1873.
1134.	„	F / V	„	1873.
1135.	„	S ♥ F	„	1873.
1136.	„	G V	„	1872.
1137.	„	M / ÆF	„	1873.
1138.	„	ME	„	1873.
1139.	„	M / I W	„	1873.
1140.	„	M / ◇B	„	1874.
1141.	„	F / I ◇ B	„	1873.
1142.	„	N H	„	1865.
1143.	„	R / I G C	„	1885.
1144.	„	R R	„	1867.
1145.	„	R ◇ S	„	1870.
1146.	„	F / W	„	1874.
1147.	„	Y S / I M	„	1879.
1148.	„	I P / I M	„	1879.
1149.	„	D / WF	„	1883.
1150.	„	M G	„	1880.
1151.	„	J M / B V	„	1880.
1152.	„	C / J M G	„	1884.
1153.	„	K O / C H	„	1884.
1154.	„	D R / I R	„	1880.

1155.	Mark	W V L H White	Crop, 1881.		1159.	Mark	S S T White	Crop, 1885.
1156.	,,	P N H White	,, 1886.		1160.	,,	C  G White	,, 1885.
1157.	,,	A H S White	,, 1882.		1161.	,,	F ◇ G White	,, 1881.
1158.	,,	B W White	,, 1877.		1162.	,,	L C G White	,, 1885.

THE

JAMAICA COURT

AT THE

𝕴𝖓𝖉𝖎𝖆𝖓 𝖆𝖓𝖉 𝕮𝖔𝖑𝖔𝖓𝖎𝖆𝖑 𝕰𝖝𝖍𝖎𝖇𝖎𝖙𝖎𝖔𝖓,

1886.

HANDBOOK

COMPILED FOR

THE GOVERNORS OF THE JAMAICA INSTITUTE

BY

LAURENCE R. FYFE

AND

A. C. SINCLAIR,

COMPILERS OF THE OFFICIAL "HANDBOOK OF JAMAICA."

CONTENTS.

....

		PAGE
Situation, Area and General Description ...	...	85
Population ...		40
History		41
Constitution and Government		46
Law and Police	...	48
Taxation	...	49
Religion and Education ...		49
Public Health		52
Trade	...	53
Productions		57
Public Gardens and Plantations ...	...	62
Lands	...	63
Postal and Telegraphic Communications ...	...	64
Means of Communication ...	...	65
Points of Topographical Interest		66
Provident and other Societies ...	...	70
Natural History	...	71
The Climate of Jamaica, by Dr. Phillippo	...	79
Jamaica, as a Winter Residence for Northern People, by Consul Hoskinson	...	88
Jamaica, as a Health Resort and as a Place to settle in, by Rev. Dr. Robb	...	92
Climate of the Santa Cruz Mountains, by Dr. Clark ...	...	97
The Climate of the Hills of Manchester, by Rev. H. Walder	...	100

C

GENERAL SIR HENRY WYLIE NORMAN,

K.C.B., C.I.E.,

GOVERNOR OF JAMAICA.

THE ISLAND OF JAMAICA.

JAMAICA, the aboriginal name of which was Xaymaca, implies the
land of streams. Bridges, the historian, is of opinion that the word
is derived from two Indian words, "Chabaüan," signifying water, and
"Makia," wood. The compound word would approach to "Chab-
makia," and harmonised to the Spanish ear would be "Cha-makia,"
thence corrupted to "Jamaica "—"denoting a land covered with wood,
and therefore watered by shaded rivulets, or, in other words, fertile."

I.—SITUATION, AREA, GENERAL DESCRIPTION, AND POPULATION.

The Island of Jamaica, which is one of the four islands which
constitute what are known as the "Greater Antilles," is situated
between 17° 43' and 18° 32' N. lat. and 76° 11' and 78° 20' 50" W.
long. It is on all sides bounded by the Caribbean Sea, the waters of
which mingle with those of the Atlantic Ocean. It is about 5,000
miles from England, 100 miles from Hayti, 90 miles from the south
of Cuba, and about 540 miles from Colon on the Isthmus of Panama.

Jamaica is 4,193 square miles in extent, having an extreme length
of 144 miles and an extreme width of 49 miles; its least width is
21½ miles. The island is divided into three countries and fourteen
parishes, namely :—

Parish		Square Miles	Parish		Square Miles	Parish		Square Miles
Kingston St. Andrew St. Thomas Portland	County of Surrey	7¼ 169½ 280 310⅔	St. Catherine St. Mary Clarendon St. Ann Manchester	County of Middlesex	450 229 467 464 310	St. Elizabeth Trelawny St. James Hanover Westmoreland	County of Cornwall	471 332½ 227¾ 166 308½
Total . .		767½	Total . .		1,920	Total . . .		1,505½

The foundation or basis of the island is composed of igneous
rocks, overlaying which are several distinct formations.

The coast formation of the parishes forming the county of Surrey
is of white and yellow limestone; the interior consists chiefly of the

metamorphosed and trappean series, with carbonaceous shales and conglomerate. The greater part of this country is very mountainous ; the only flats are the plain of Liguanea (north of Kingston) and the valleys of the Morant and Plantain Garden rivers, and smaller flats at and near the mouths of the other chief rivers. Mineral deposits are numerous in the mountain districts. Iron, copper, lead, manganese, and cobalt have been found and worked to some extent, but no profitable industry has been the result. Marble of good quality has also been found at the head of the Blue Mountain valley.

In the county of Middlesex the parish of St. Mary exhibits a great diversity of formation, consisting of white and yellow limestone, carbonaceous shales, metamorphosed, porphyritic, granite, and conglomerate rocks, with many mineral-bearing rocks. The district of St. Thomas-in-the-Vale is of granitic formation, overlaid considerably by cretaceous and white limestone and marl beds. St. Catherine possesses an extensive alluvial flat, stretching from Kingston harbour to the boundary of Clarendon; the rest of the parish is of white limestone. In Upper Clarendon the metamorphosed trappean and conglomerate series prevail ; the central districts are of white limestone, and the southern part, with the district of Vere, is alluvium, and embraces an area of about 132 square miles, which is the largest continuous flat in the island. The mineral deposits of Upper Clarendon are considerable, and it is believed offer a fair field for mining enterprise. The parishes of Manchester and St. Ann consist almost entirely of white limestone.

The parish of St. Elizabeth, in the county of Cornwall, has an extensive area of alluvium from the boundary of Manchester to the boundary of Westmoreland, narrowing so considerably at Lacovia that the north and south limestones nearly meet ; much of this flat is covered by swamp. In the north-east of the parish there is also an extensive flat called the Nassau Valley. The rest of the parish is white limestone, with some patches of yellow limestone. The parish of Westmoreland also presents extensive alluvial deposits and marl beds. The north-western part of the parish furnishes trappean rocks with yellow and cretaceous limestone. The eastern part is chiefly white limestone, with some trap formations at the head of the Great River. In Trelawny the district called the "Black Grounds" consists of trap formation. The rest of the parish is of white limestone, with some alluvial valleys; that called the "Queen of Spain's Valley," on the borders of St. James, is remarkable for its picturesque beauty and great fertility. The interior of St. James presents a trappean formation, with some over-laying yellow and cretaceous limestones. The rest is of white limestone, with some alluvial deposits round the coast. The eastern part of Hanover is chiefly white limestone, and the western part black shale, with some metamorphosed rocks and yellow limestone.

The surface of the island is extremely mountainous, and attains considerable altitudes. A great diversity of climate is, therefore, obtainable. From a tropical temperature of 80° to 86° at the sea-coast, the thermometer falls to 45° and 50° on the top of the highest mountains, and with a dryness of atmosphere that renders the climate of the mountains of Jamaica particularly delightful and suitable to the most delicate constitutions. Ice has been quite recently found on the top of the Blue Mountains.*

The mountains in the midland part of the island are the highest. Through the county of Surrey and partly through Middlesex there runs the great central chain which trends generally in an east and west direction, the highest part of which is the Blue Mountain Peak, attaining an elevation of 7,360 feet.

The following are the elevations above the sea of the principal mountains and passes :—

Names	Elevation in feet	Names	Elevation in feet
John Crow Range, average .	2,100	Silver Hill Gap . . .	3,513
Cuna-Cuna Pass . . .	2,698	Catherine's Peak . . .	5,036
Blue Mountain, Western Peak.	7,360	Cold Spring Gap . . .	4,523
Portland Gap	5,549	Hardware Gap . . .	4,079
Sir John's Peak (highest point } of Cinchona Plantation) }	6,100	Fox's Gap	3,967
Belle Vue, Cinchona Plantation	5,017	Stony Hill (where main road } crosses it) }	1,360
Arntully Gap	2,754	Guy's Hill	2,100
Hagley Gap	1,959	Mount Diablo, highest point	2,300
Morce's Gap	4,945	„ „ where road crosses	1,800
Content Gap	3,251	Bull Head	2,885
Newcastle Hospital . .	3,800	Mandeville	2,131
Flamstead	3,663	Accompong Town . . .	1,409
Belle Vue (Dr. Stephens') .	3,784	Dolphin Head . . .	1,816

The numerous rivers and springs which abound along the coast in most parts of the island to a considerable extent justify the name of " the Land of Springs," although there are extensive districts in the midland and western parts of the island singularly barren of water.

---

* As affording the most reliable information as to the climate of Jamaica, papers are annexed to this Handbook, forming Appendices A, B, C, D, and E, entitled "The Climate of Jamaica," by Dr. Phillippo, a Physician of great experience, resident in Kingston ; " Jamaica as a winter residence for Northern People," by Mr. E. Hoskinson, for many years Consul at Kingston for the United States of America; "Jamaica as a Health Resort," by the Rev. Dr. Robb, Principal of the Presbyterian Training College, Kingston ; " The Climate of the Santa Cruz Mountains," by Dr. J. H. Clark, the District Medical Officer for that District, and the " Climate of the Manchester Mountains," by the Rev. H. Walder, Moravian Missionary.

In consequence of the great elevations from which most of the rivers flow, they are very rapid in their descent, and in times of flood become formidable torrents, sweeping everything before them, and operating as dangerous obstructions to the traveller.

The chief rivers are the Agua Alta or Wag Water, running through the parishes of St. Andrew and St. Mary; the Hope River, in the parish of St. Andrew; the Rio Cobre, running through the parish of St. Catherine; the Plantain Garden, Morant and Yallahs, rivers in the parish of St. Thomas; the Rio Grande, the Swift, the Spanish and Buff Bay rivers, in the parish of Portland; the Cave River, forming the boundary between the parishes of St. Ann and Clarendon; the Hector's River, dividing the parish of Trelawny from Manchester the Rio Minho, or Dry River, and the Milk River, in the parish of Clarendon; the Black River, in the parish of St. Elizabeth; the Martha Bræ River, in the parish of Trelawny; the Cabaritta River, in the parish of Westmoreland; and the Great River, dividing the parishes of St. James and Hanover. The Black River, in the parish of St. Elizabeth, is navigable for thirty miles of its course. The water is fresh from three to five miles up the river according to the season of the year. None of the other rivers of the island are navigable even to the extent stated above.

The principal ports are Kingston and Port Royal, in the parish of Kingston; Old Harbour Bay, in St. Catherine; Salt River and Carlisle Bay, in Clarendon; Alligator Pond, in Manchester; Black River, in St. Elizabeth; Savanna-la-Mar, in Westmoreland; Lucea, in Hanover; Montego Bay, in St. James; Falmouth and Rio Bueno, in Trelawny; Dry Harbour and St. Ann's Bay, in St. Ann; Port Maria and Annotto Bay, in St. Mary; Port Antonio, Buff Bay, and Manchioneal, in Portland; Port Morant and Morant Bay, in St. Thomas.

The chief bays are Morant Bay, Old Harbour Bay, Carlisle Bay, Alligator Pond Bay, Black River Bay, Negril Bay, Montego Bay, St. Ann's Bay, Ocho Rios Bay, Annotto Bay, Buff Bay, Hope Bay, and Plantain Garden River Bay.

The principal capes or promontories are Morant Point, in the parish of St. Thomas; Portland Point, in Clarendon; Great Pedro Bluff and Parotte Point, in St. Elizabeth; Negril Point, in Westmoreland; Montego Bay Point, in St. James, and Galina Point, in St. Mary.

There are many mineral springs in the island possessing valuable qualities for the cure of various diseases. The spring at Bath, in the parish of St. Thomas, is the hottest in the island; the temperature at the fountain head is 126° to 128° F., but the water loses about 9°

of heat in its transit to the baths. These waters are sulphuric and contain a large proportion of hydro-sulphate of lime; they are not purgative, and are beneficial in gout, rheumatism, gravelly complaints, cutaneous affections, and fevers. A cold spring flows from the same hillside, near the hot spring, so that cold and hot water are delivered alongside of each other at the bath.

The bath at Milk River, in the district of Vere, is one of the most remarkable in the world. It is a warm, saline, purgative bath; the temperature is 92° F. It is particularly efficacious in the cure of gout, rheumatism, paralysis, and neuralgia; also in cases of disordered liver and spleen. Some wonderful results are on record, and it is believed that if the beneficial effects of these waters were more generally known in Europe and America a large number of sufferers would be attracted to them.

The waters of the Spa Spring, or Jamaica Spa as it is called, at Silver Hill, in St. Andrew, are chalybeate, aërated, cold, and tonic, and are beneficial in most cases of debility, particularly after fever, dropsy and in stomach complaints.

There is also a remarkable spring at Moffat, on the White River, a tributary of the Negro River in the Blue Mountain Valley. These waters are sulphuric, cold, and purgative, useful in itch and all cutaneous diseases. A similar spring exists near the source of the Cabaritta River, in Hanover.

The chief towns of Jamaica are Kingston, which is the largest and most important commercial town in the British West Indies, and forms the capital of the parish known by that name; Spanish Town, in the parish of St. Catherine; Chapelton, in the parish of Clarendon; Mandeville, in the parish of Manchester; Black River, in the parish of St. Elizabeth; Savanna-la-Mar, in the parish of Westmoreland; Lucea, in the parish of Hanover; Montego Bay, in the parish of St. James; Falmouth, in the parish of Trelawny; St. Ann's Bay, in the parish of St. Ann; Port Maria, in the parish of St. Mary; Port Antonio, in the parish of Portland; and Morant Bay, in the parish of St. Thomas.

Kingston, which was built after the destruction of Port Royal by the earthquake of 1692, is now the seat of Government. It is lighted with gas, and has a constant and abundant supply of wholesome water; it is the head station of the Jamaica Railway, and has very excellent lines of tram cars traversing the principal streets. It is the centre of the telegraphic lines of the West India and Panama Telegraph Company and of the Government Inland System, and is the chief seaport of the island. It contains fourteen churches, a number of schools, a town hall, a theatre, two court houses, a number of well-kept hotels and lodging-houses, and the colonial secretariat and other public offices. In the suburbs are the lunatic asylum, the public hospital, and the general penitentiary. A remarkably handsome and very commodious market adorns the lower end of King Street. Near the pier, which forms part of the market buildings, is a well-executed marble statue of Admiral Lord Rodney, who defeated Count de Grasse in his descent on the British West Indies in April 1782. In the upper part of the same street, and on the east and north sides of the public garden, are statues respectively of Sir Charles Theophilus Metcalfe, a former Governor of the island, the Honourable Edward Jordon, C.B., one of Jamaica's most distinguished sons, and Dr. Lewis Quier Bowerbank, an eminent physician and a great sanitary reformer. Around the city proper have grown up a large number of tasteful and commodious villas, ornamented with shrubberies and gardens. The rent of good and commodious houses in Kingston is from £50 to £100 a year; the direct taxes amount to 3s. 10d. per head of the population. Five daily newspapers are published in Kingston.

The population of Jamaica in the years 1861, 1871, and 1881, as ascertained by the census taken in each of those years, was 441,264, 506,154, and 580,804 respectively; showing an increase of 64,890 between 1861 and 1871, and an increase of 74,650 between 1871 and 1881; the increase for the 20 years between 1861 and 1881 having been 139,540.

The population in 1881 was thus classified in the census returns:—

Males	282,957
Females	297,874
	580,804
White	14,432
Coloured	109,946
Black	444,186
Coolie	11,016
Chinese	99
Not stated	1,125
	580,804

The estimated population in the years subsequent to 1881 is as follows:—

1882	588,718	1884		591,819
1883	594,023	1885		596,383

The natural increase of population for the whole island during the year 1885 over 1884 was 15·5 per 1,000 persons living.

The following is the population of the chief towns as shown by

the census returns of 1881. Since then the population of the island
has considerably increased, as indicated above, so that the population
of the towns, as given below, must be regarded as merely approximate
as regards the present time :—

Kingston	...	...	...	36,522	Lucea	... ...	1,702
Spanish Town	...	...		5,689	Montego Bay...	... ...	4,651
Chapelton	...	...	...	654	Falmouth	... ...	3,029
Mandeville	...	...	...	218	St. Ann's Bay	... ...	1,565
Black River	...	...	...	1,279	Port Maria	... ...	6,741
Savanna-la-Mar	...	...		2,498	Port Antonio...	... ...	1,305
	Morant Bay	...	...	...	...	1,000	

II.—History.

Jamaica was discovered by Christopher Columbus on May 3,
1494, and remained in Spanish possession until May 11, 1655,
when it capitulated to an English expedition commanded by Admiral
Penn and General Venables. The island was placed under military
jurisdiction and continued so until May 1661, when a commission was
received from Charles II. appointing General D'Oyley Governor, and
authorising him to govern by means of an elected Council. Courts of
Law were established, and the members of Council were declared
Justices of the Peace and empowered to appoint Constables for their
respective districts. In December of the same year the King, by a
Royal Proclamation, declared that "children born in Jamaica of Her
Majesty's natural born subjects of England shall be free denizens of
England." In August 1662, Lord Windsor arrived as the successor
of D'Oyley and brought with him additional instructions as to the
government of the country. The army was disbanded and a militia
established and ordinances were passed for the encouragement of
religious liberty and toleration. In January 1663, the first General
Assembly was held, and a body of laws was passed which was declared
by a contemporary historian to be " as good as could be expected from
such young statesmen."

Sir Thomas Modyford arrived as Governor in June 1664, and
settled the seat of Government at Spanish Town. He brought with
him a thousand persons, to whom he granted lands in the interior ; and,
as they were possessed of means, they soon began planting to the great
benefit of the colony. He had acquired a large fortune by planting
operations in Barbados, and he now freely expended his wealth in the
same direction in Jamaica. He instructed the inhabitants "in the
manner of making sugar, of planting cacao groves, of managing
pimento walks, and of erecting salt works."* The result was the

---

* "History of Barbados," by Power.

increased value of the products and the extension of cultivation. Cacao was then considered " the best commodity in the island. A planter obtained from 20 acres of cacao plants 12 cwts. of nuts, which he sold in England for £8. 12s. per cwt." The best sugar works made at that time 20,000 to 30,000 lbs. of sugar a week, which were sold for 50 per cent. beyond Barbados sugar.*

Sir Thomas Modyford, in his first report to the King, stated that " sugar, ginger, indigo, cotton, tobacco, dyeing woods, and cacao were produced in Jamaica as well as elsewhere, but there were numerous other commodities ; the best building timber and stone in the whole world, plenty of corn, potatoes, yams, cattle, horses, fowl, sheep, fruit, and pasturage. In short, nothing was then wanting but more hands and cows."† The former were secured by the Royal African Company being required at a moderate rate to supply the island with slaves from the Coast of Africa, and by the King ordering that all felons convicted in the Circuit Courts and at the Old Bailey, whose sentences might be commuted to transportation, being sent to Jamaica. The King also engaged to pay from the Imperial Exchequer for one year the cost of emigration from Barbados and the Leeward Islands. The required cattle were obtained from the Cape de Verde Islands, Hispanniola, and Cuba. The price paid for the supply from the two last-named places was 4s. per head.

With the view of encouraging immigration to the colony, the King ordered Sir Thomas Modyford to be prodigal in the granting of lands allowing 30 acres per head to men, women, and children, white and black. All patentees were, however, required to begin cultivation within three years, and to pay a fine of 1s. per acre on all lands left unplanted after that period.

Privateers at that time swarmed the Caribbean Sea, and Sir Thomas Modyford legalised their actions and utilised their services by commissioning them to act on behalf of the King of England " against Spain and all nationalities." The privateers thereupon seized Tobago and other places in the Atlantic, and eventually captured and pillaged Panama, in the Pacific. On intelligence of these proceedings reaching England, Sir Thomas Modyford was ordered to be sent " under a strong and safe guard " to England to answer for his assumption of power, and his commissions to the privateers were annulled. The colony, however, continued to grow rich, and in 1675 it exported " vast quantities of sugar, superior to that of the other islands." The population had by this time greatly increased, as it numbered 7,768 free people and 9,504 slaves.

* " Calendar of State Papers," vol. ii. † Ibid.

The political dissensions between the Governor and the Assembly, which began during the administration of Sir Thomas Modyford, now produced a political dead-lock, and left the colony without a revenue. To prevent a continuation of these legislative conflicts the Earl of Carlisle (who assumed the government in June 1678) was directed to introduce into the island the Irish mode of legislation as laid down in Poynings' Act; but so persistent and determined was the opposition of the Assembly that the King had to restore the old form of government and to recall the Earl of Carlisle.

On June 7, 1692, the great earthquake occurred by which almost the whole of Port Royal was destroyed. " Whole streets, with their inhabitants, were swallowed up by the opening of the earth, which as it closed again squeezed the people to death, and in that manner several were left with their heads above ground."* Of the 3,000 houses, which the town possessed, only about 200, with Fort Charles, remained uninjured.

Two years later a French fleet, commanded by Admiral Du Casse (acting in the interest of the fugitive King), landed in the eastern and southern parts of the island, and by horrid atrocities secured a large amount of money. They took several merchant ships, destroyed 50 plantations, and carried off 1,300 slaves. They were encountered at Salt River by the Colonial Militia, and driven back to their ships with the loss of 700 men. This was the only battle fought on Jamaica ground with a foreign enemy after the expulsion of the Spaniards.

In 1760 a premeditated rebellion occurred among the slaves in St. Mary. The insurgents seized the fort at Port Maria, and possessed themselves of arms, ammunition, and other stores. The white inhabitants of the neighbouring properties were all butchered, and the rebels retired to Ballard's Valley, where they gave battle to a body of volunteers. They fought with desperate fury, but they were surrounded and overpowered. More than 400 were killed in the field, and about 600 were transported to the Bay of Honduras. This was the most formidable slave insurrection in the history of the colony.

In 1795 the Trelawny Town Maroons expelled their European Superintendent, and threatened to march upon Montego Bay and commit reprisals for the flogging by order of the Magistrates of two of their people. A detachment of 400 soldiers was despatched to subdue the insurgents, but they were met by volley after volley from unseen hands. Fresh detachments were despatched, but they met

---

* Bridge's " Annals of Jamaica."

with no better success; they, too, fell into ambuscade, and were almost exterminated. The conflict continued for months, and was only brought to a close by the introduction of Spanish blood-hounds to trace out and destroy the insurgents in the forests. The Maroons capitulated, and were transported to Sierra Leone, where they formed the nucleus of that thriving colony.

In the year 1807 the African slave trade was abolished; and in the following year the government of the Duke of Manchester (which lasted for 19 years) began. During the administration of the Duke of Manchester, the Assembly was called upon by the Imperial Government to enact laws for the amelioration of the condition of the slaves. This was regarded by the House as an interference with their constitutional rights, and they rejected every suggestion made to them. The result was a conflict between the Imperial Government and the House of Assembly, during which "the slave-owners threatened to transfer their allegiance to the United States, or to assert their independence after the manner of their continental neighbours." The excitement which these proceedings produced extended itself to the slave population, and resulted in an outbreak on December 28, 1831. A number of the insurgents were killed in the field; several of the ringleaders were captured, tried, and executed; and the remainder returned to the estates. Property of the value of £666,977 sterling was destroyed by the insurgents; and the Imperial Government, in commiseration of the deplorable state to which the proprietors were reduced, extended to them a loan of £200,000 to replenish their plantations. This rebellion culminated in the entire abolition of slavery in the British Possessions. The Jamaica slave-owners received £5,853,975 sterling as compensation for the 255,290 able-bodied negroes who were emancipated.

In the year 1838 (the year of emancipation) the value of the sugar, rum, and coffee exported was £1,455,185. From that time the exports of the staples continued to decline; but in 1842 the Earl of Elgin arrived as Governor, and he distinguished his government by his efforts to improve the social condition of the colony, and to develop its varied industrial resources. A Royal Agricultural Society, and several parochial associations of a similar kind, were established under his presidency; and a variety of improvements in modes of cultivation, machinery, &c., were introduced through his instrumentality. Immigration from India was authorised by the Imperial Government, and the first batch of Coolies arrived in 1845. Attention was also directed to the cultivation of the minor products; but the beneficial effects of these important improvements were soon to be displaced by despondency and retrogression. In August 1846 the

Imperial Parliament passed an Act for the gradual equalisation of the sugar duties on British and Foreign productions, and the Assembly, in the succeeding November, declared that "they were, in consequence, unable to continue the institutions of the colony on their present scale, or to defray the future expense of Coolie immigration." The result was the immediate cessation of immigration, and a struggle between the Assembly and the Council for a general reduction of the salaries of all public officers, which continued for 13 years, and which ended in the loss of £130,000 of revenue, and a change in the form of government.

The new government was inaugurated by Governor Sir Henry Barkly in October 1853, and the Legislature passed laws for effecting financial reforms and restoring public credit. But this desirable state of accord did not long continue, as Sir Charles Darling's interpretation of the Act for the better government of the island introduced ministerial responsibility, and with this a constant struggle for place and power. These political dissensions continued during the government of Mr. Edward John Eyre, who succeeded Sir Charles Darling, until everybody's attention was directed to more serious events. An outbreak occurred at Morant Bay on October 11, 1865, during which the Custos of the parish and several Magistrates, a number of the officers and men of the Volunteers, and the Curate of Bath, were killed. The immediate despatch of a military force to the scene of disturbance, and the loyalty of the greater part of the prædial classes, secured the early restoration of order. Martial law was, however, continued for a month, during which Mr. George William Gordon, one of the representatives in the House of Assembly for St. Thomas-in-the-East, and a number of the ringleaders of the outbreak, were tried by Court-Martial and executed; others were flogged, and a number were sentenced to penal servitude. A Royal Commission of Inquiry, which was subsequently sent to the island, reported that the disturbances had their immediate origin in a planned resistance to lawful authority; but that the punishments were excessive, and, in some cases, positively barbarous. Governor Eyre was recalled, and Sir John Peter Grant (formerly Lieutenant-Governor of Bengal) was commissioned as Governor. During his administration the provisions of the law which was passed by the Legislature (after the disturbance above briefly recorded) for abolishing representative government in the colony were brought into effect, and Jamaica was declared a Crown colony. After a lapse of 18 years, this form of government was modified by the introduction of the elective element into the Legislative Council. This change was effected on the assumption of the government by Governor Sir Henry Wylie Norman, who continues to administer the government, enjoying the confidence and esteem of all classes of the community.

III.—CONSTITUTION AND GOVERNMENT.

The Local Legislature of Jamaica passed two laws in the month of December 1865, by which the then Legislative Council and House of Assembly were abolished and the Queen was empowered " to create and constitute a Government for this island, in such form and with such powers as to Her Majesty might seem fitting, and from time to time to alter or amend such Government." In pursuance of these enactments a single Chamber was established under the designation of " the Legislative Council of Jamaica." The Council thus created consisted of the Senior Military Officer for the time being in command of the regular troops in the island, the Colonial Secretary and the Attorney-General, by virtue of their offices, and such other officers and persons as Her Majesty might think fit to appoint as official and unofficial members of the Board.

The entire body of unofficial members resigned their seats in November 1882, in consequence of the passing of a resolution by the votes of the official members directing the payment from colonial funds of one-half of the damages and costs in the suit for the seizure of the schooner " Florence," by order of the Governor. (There was then one vacancy in the number of unofficial members, and two were absent from the island.) Petitions were forwarded from the inhabitants of the principal towns to the Imperial Government in support of the action taken by the unofficial members, and praying for the remodelling of the Political Constitution of the colony. The consequence was the passing of an Order by the Queen in Council, dated May 19, 1884, in which it was declared that a new Legislative Council should be constituted, which should consist of the Governor, the Senior Military Officer for the time being in command of Her Majesty's regular troops in Jamaica, the Colonial Secretary, the Attorney-General, and the Director of Public Works ; not more than five members nominated by the Crown, and nine members elected by taxpayers of 20s. and upwards. The island was by the said Order in Council divided into nine electoral districts, and a member apportioned to each.

With the view of granting to the elected members substantial power and responsibility in legislation, it was provided in the Order in Council that where six elected members were agreed on a question affecting finances the *ex-officio* and nominated members should not be required to vote ; and where the nine elected members were agreed on any other question the same rule should be observed with regard to the votes of the *ex-officio* and nominated members. As a further concession to the elective element on the inauguration of the new system of government, only two nominated members were appointed—namely, the Superintending Medical Officer and the Inspector of Schools—thus practically giving a majority of three elected members in the Legislative Council.

The Governor of the island is President of the Legislative Council, and six members and the President constitute a quorum for the dispatch of business. Any member may propose any question for debate unless it involves the raising or expending of revenue—this latter power being vested in the Governor alone.

There is also a Privy Council consisting of the Senior Military Officer, the Colonial Secretary, the Attorney-General, and such other persons, not exceeding eight in number, as may be appointed by the Queen. The only appointed member at present is Major-General Mann, Director of Public Works. " The Governor is to consult in all cases with the Privy Councillors, excepting only when the matter to be decided would in his judgment sustain material prejudice by consultation or be too unimportant to require their advice."

The following is a list of the Legislative Council as at present constituted :—

Ex-Officio and Nominated Members.

His Excellency Sir Henry Wylie Norman, K.C.B., C.I.E., Governor, President.

The Hon. Major-General Somerset Molyneux Wiseman-Clarke, Commander of the Forces.

Hon. E. N. Walker, C.M.G., Colonial Secretary.

Hon. Henry H. Hocking, Attorney-General.

Hon. Major-General J. R. Mann, R.E., C.M.G., Director of Public Works.

Hon. Deputy Surgeon-General C. B. Mosse, C.B., Superintending Medical Officer.

Hon. Thos. Capper, Inspector of Schools.

Elected Members.

Hon. Charles Salmon Farquharson, for Westmoreland and Hanover.

Hon. James Miller Farquharson, for St. Elizabeth.

Hon. George Henderson, for Portland and St. Thomas.

Hon. Robert Craig, for Clarendon.

Hon. Emanuel George Levy, for St. Catherine.

Hon. William Malabre, for Kingston and St. Andrew.

Hon. John Thomson Palache, for Manchester.

Hon. Michael Solomon, for St. Ann and St. Mary.

Hon. Wellesley Bourke, for St. James and Trelawny.

Previous to the admission of the elective element into the Legislative Council, the Municipal Boards and the Road Boards were annually appointed by the Governor on the recommendation of the Custodes of parishes. These Boards discharged the parochial duties performed by the elected Vestries and the old Commissioners of Highways and Bridges previous to the abolition, in 1865, of the then Constitution.

Since the recent change in the constitution of the Legislative Council the Municipal Boards and the Road Boards have been abolished, and a Parochial Board has been established in each parish, consisting of the person representing the electoral district in the Legislative Council, the Custos of the parish, and from 13 to 18 persons elected by the taxpayers who are qualified to vote at elections for the Legislative Council. In Kingston the Chairman of the Board is styled Mayor, and the members are styled Councillors. The Parochial Boards manage all the local affairs that have hitherto been discharged by the Municipal and Road Boards.

The estimates of the parochial expenditure are prepared by the Parochial Boards under sanction of the Governor. These, with the estimates of public expenditure, which are prepared by the Colonial Secretary, under the instructions of the Governor, are annually presented to the Legislative Council in the form of a Minute from the Governor. After all the items are considered by the Council, they are incorporated in an Appropriation Law, the schedule of which becomes the Civil List of the year.

IV.—LAW AND POLICE.

The Judicial Establishment consists of a Supreme Court of Judicature, an Admiralty Court, District Courts, and Courts of Petty Sessions.

The Supreme Court has incorporated with it the High Court of Chancery, the Incumbered Estates Court, the Court of Ordinary, the Court of Divorce and Matrimonial Causes, the Chief Court of Bankruptcy, and the Circuit Courts. The several divisions of the Supreme Court, except the Circuit Courts, sit in Kingston at times appointed by the Judges. For the purpose of the sitting of the Circuit Courts the island is divided into parochial districts. There are a Chief Justice and two Assistant-Judges, who divide the duties of the Supreme Court by arrangements among themselves.

The Court of Admiralty has an organisation of its own. It is a branch of the Admiralty Court of England. The matters in respect to which this Court exercises jurisdiction particularly relate to seamen, pilotage, salvage, damages by ships, &c. It sits whenever there is business to be disposed of.

For the purposes of the District Courts the island is divided into six districts, consisting of adjacent localities. There are five District Court Judges—the Junior Assistant-Judge of the Supreme Court presiding in the Civil Division of the City of Kingston District Court. A District Court Judge presides in each of the other District Courts.

Courts of Petty Sessions are held in the several parishes, and are presided over by Stipendiary or Local Magistrates.

The Attorney-General and two Assistants act as Public Prosecutors.

Barristers, Advocates, and Solicitors practise in the several Courts of the island.

The Police Force consists of 18 Inspectors and Sub-Inspectors, and 673 Sub-Officers and Constables; 19 Water Policemen, and 1,080 Rural Policemen. They are under the command of an Inspector-General of Police.

There are a General Penitentiary, two Gaols, and six other Prisons in different parts of the island. A Government Reformatory for boys is maintained at Stony Hill and one for girls at Admirals' Pen, in St. Andrew.

V.—TAXATION.

The principal heads of general revenue are import duties, excise, and stamps. Taxes on houses, wheels, and horsekind are imposed for parochial purposes. The revenue received for public or general purposes during the financial year ending September 30, 1885, amounted to £504,718, and for local or parochial purposes to £90,437 ; total, £595,155. The expenditure during the same period was, for general purposes, £470,353, and for local purposes, £92,348 ; total, £562,701.

The rate of taxation·was 16s. 11d. per head of the population for general purposes and 3s. per head for local purposes, making a total of 19s. 11d. per head.

VI.—RELIGION AND EDUCATION.

There is no Ecclesiastical Establishment in the island, the Church of England in Jamaica having been disestablished in 1869.

D

The Church of England, or Episcopal Church in Jamaica, now numbers 1 Bishop, 60 Rectors, and 22 Curates—total, 83. These Clergymen, assisted by Catechists and Lay Readers, officiate at 101 churches and chapels. The last returns showed a total of 29,080 registered members. The total revenue of the Church for the year 1884 was £27,484. The capital funds amounted in the year 1884 to £55,725. There were 228 Elementary Schools in connection with the Episcopal Church in Jamaica.

The Established Church of Scotland in Jamaica has 3 Clergymen, who are stationed in Kingston, St. Elizabeth, and Manchester, and about 1,500 communicants. There are 9 Elementary Schools in connection with this Church.

The Roman Catholics have 29 stations and an accredited membership of 9,292. These stations include the Convent of the Immaculate Conception in Kingston, to which twelve Sisters of the Order of St. Francis are attached. A Boarding School, a Middle-Class Day School, and an Elementary Day School are kept by the Ladies of the Convent. There are 11 other Elementary Schools attached to the Roman Catholic Church, besides St. George's College, in North Street, Kingston, for the higher education of Catholic boys. The Vicar Apostolic and 11 other priests form the Clergy of the Roman Catholic community in Jamaica; they are all of the Society of Jesus.

The Wesleyans have 192 Chapels and other preaching places, 31 Ministers, 19,264 members, and 1,084 probationers. Their organisation is now styled "The Western Annual Conference." Their Day Schools number 101, and their Sabbath Schools 103. The former include the Colleges for boys at York Castle, in St. Ann, and for girls at Barbican, in St. Andrew.

The Baptist Missionary Society has 130 Churches and 56 Ministers. The total number of communicants is 30,000, and the number of inquirers 4,467. There are 92 Sunday Schools, with a roll of 1,407 teachers and 15,407 scholars. The Day Schools number 137, with an average attendance of 5,918 pupils. Calabar College, for the education and training of Ministers attached to this Mission, is situated in East Queen Street, Kingston.

The United Presbyterian Church in Jamaica numbers 43 regular Churches and 27 out-stations; these are scattered over 10 of the parishes of the island. Thirty-one Missionaries, 8,577 communicants, and 1,435 candidates for Church Communion are attached to this body. They have 628 Sunday-School Classes, with 662 teachers and 6,462 scholars. The Presbyterians have a Theological College in

Kingston, where the candidates for their Ministry are educated and trained; and they have 75 Elementary Schools in different localities, the larger number being in the parishes of St. Mary and Manchester.

The United Methodists' Free Churches have 34 stations and 9 Ministers. The membership numbers 3,081 communicants and 251 probationers. They have 32 Elementary Schools in connection with their Society.

The London Missionary Society has 15 Churches and a number of out-stations and cottage meeting-houses; 8 Pastors and 9 Catechists. There are 2,927 accredited Church members and 761 candidates and inquirers, with an attendance of about 1,669 pupils at the Sunday Schools. The Elementary Day Schools number 22, and are principally in Clarendon.

The Christian Church, or "The Disciples of Christ," have 15 Churches, with a membership of about 1,500. These Churches are served by 7 Ministers. They have 8 Elementary Schools under Government inspection.

The Moravian Church has 14 principal stations and 5 out-stations; they are all at the western end of the island, principally in Manchester, St. Elizabeth, and Westmoreland. The number of communicants at the close of 1884 was 5,603, with 15,765 persons in Church connection. There were 64 Schools, with 4,886 children attending them. There is a Training School for Male Teachers at Fairfield, in Manchester, and a similar Institution for Female Teachers at Bethabara, in the same parish. At the close of 1884 there were 12 ordained Missionaries in the Moravian Church in Jamaica in charge of congregations.

There is a Government Training College in Spanish Town which sends out an average of 8 trained Masters annually; the number of Students now in residence is 31.

There is also a Government Training College at Camperdown Pen, in St. Andrew, for Female Teachers; there are 21 Lady Students. There is likewise a Training College for 30 Male Students at the Mico, in Kingston. These institutions are strictly undenominational.

There are several Endowed Schools in the island where higher and middle-class education may be had either free of all charges or at nominal rates. There are the Jamaica High School, in St. Andrew, the Mico and Wolmer's, in Kingston, Titchfield and Merrick's, in Portland, Munro and Dickenson's, in St. Elizabeth, Rusea's, in Hanover, the Vere and Manchester Free-Schools, in Clarendon and

Manchester, Smith and Beckford's, in St. Catherine, and Manning's, in Westmoreland.

There are also a number of Private Schools where a superior education may be obtained. The Church of England and Collegiate High School and the Mary Villa College, in Kingston, are among the leading schools of this class for boys; the same remark applying to the Wesleyan High School at York Castle, in St. Ann's, for boys, and to the Wesleyan High School for girls at Barbican, in St. Andrew.

A Government scholarship is annually granted in Jamaica; it is confined to boys born in Jamaica, or of parents domiciled in Jamaica, and resident there for five years preceding the day of examination. This scholarship is of the value of £200 per annum for three years, and enables the successful competitor to obtain a University education in Great Britain.

In furtherance of education there is a public library in Kingston, consisting of scientific, historical, and general literature. A large collection of school books is included in these volumes. A museum is attached to the institute, and lectures are periodically delivered by the members and others on subjects bearing on the material interests of the country.

VII.—THE PUBLIC HEALTH.

The Medical Department consists of a staff of medical officers at the public hospital of Kingston and in the several parishes, all of whom are under the direction of the Superintending Medical Officer.

The public hospital of Kingston is situated in North Street and contains 200 beds. There are 18 public general hospitals situated in convenient localities throughout the island, in which the labourers employed on estates and the indigent poor are treated. These hospitals contain a total of 1,090 beds.

Government dispensaries are established in remote districts, at which the District Medical Officers attend on fixed days to give advice and to dispense medicines at a moderate rate of fees. A poor person, although not a pauper, who may be unable to attend at a hospital, dispensary, or at the residence of a District Medical Officer, by reason of serious illness or infirmity, is attended at his residence by the District Medical Officer of his district, under certain regulations.

The lunatic asylum is at Rae Town, in the parish of Kingston; it is the finest building of the sort in the British West Indies; it has accommodation for over 370 patients.

Quarantine regulations are strictly maintained at the several ports. There is a Lazaretto for the port of Kingston at Green Bay, opposite Port Royal; it stands on a projecting cliff overlooking the harbour, and is some 50 to 60 feet above sea-level. The buildings are capable of accommodating 68 persons.

The sanitary affairs of the island are directed and supervised by a Central Board of Health which sits in Kingston. The Parochial Boards, as the Local Boards of Health, carry out the recommendations of the Central Board. The officers and sub-officers of the Constabulary are Inspectors of Nuisances. There is a Commissioner of Health for Kingston.

VIII.—TRADE.

The value of the merchandise and other articles imported during the financial year 1885, stood thus : Value of imports from the United Kingdom, £761,157 ; from the Dominion of Canada, £177,172 ; from the United States, £464,282 ; from other countries, £58,762 ; total of imports, £1,456,373. The following represents the value of the principal articles imported : Foodstuffs, £642,500 ; clothing, £424,900; building materials, £99,800 ; household necessaries, £54.500 : furniture, £18,800 ; railway and estates supplies, £31,000 ; coal, £29,500 ; books, £9,800 ; specie, £9,600.

The export trade of the island stood thus in 1885 : Value of exports to the United Kingdom, £532,971 ; to the Dominion of Canada, £65,775 ; to the United States, £595,237 ; to other countries, £214,865 ; total, £1,408,848.

The value of the total exports for the year 1885 were below those of 1884 by £75,141. This is attributable to two causes—the severe and lengthened drought which existed almost during the entire year 1885, inducing low production and the generally depressed state of trade inducing low prices.

Sugar and rum (the principal staples of the country) stood at the head of the list of exports and in the following proportion to the total of exports : Sugar, 22 per cent. ; rum, 17 per cent. The other products came in the following order : Coffee, 11 per cent.; fruit, 11 per cent. ; dye woods, 11 per cent. ; pimento, 4 per cent.

The subjoined return shows the quantity and value of the exports during the year ended September 30, 1885. The articles were exported in the following proportions to the countries named : United

Kingdom, 37·2; United States, 42·2; Dominion of Canada, 5·4; other countries, 15·2 :—

ARTICLE	QUANTITY.	VALUE.		
		£	s.	d.
Annotto...	288,187 lbs.	3,602	6	9
Arrowroot	9 c. 0 q. 22 lbs.	13	14	6
Beeswax	1,107 c. 2 q. 9 lbs.	6,202	9	0
Cattle, neat	109 no.	1,078	0	0
Cacoa	3,028 c. 1 q. 14 lbs.	6,359	11	10
Coconnuts	5,115,872 no.	17,905	11	0
Coffee	80,657 c. 0 q. 22 lbs.	157,281	11	10
Fruit: Bananas	1,417,282 bunches	129,918	10	4
„ Limes	809¼ barrels	323	14	0
„ Mangoes	166,705 no.	161	5	0
„ Oranges	22,614,390 no.	31,660	2	11
„ Pine-apples	8,883 dozs.	1,443	9	9
„ Shaddocks	15 barrels	5	6	0
Ginger	12,313 c. 0 q. 15 lbs.	20,168	18	3
Hides	376,327 lbs.	9,408	3	6
Honey	1,311 c. 0 q. 26 lbs.	1,573	9	7
Horses and Mules	98 no.	2,039	0	0
Lance Wood Spars	6,685 no.	2,005	10	0
Limejuice	54,934 galls.	2,060	0	6
Pimento	87,447 c. 0 q. 14 lbs.	53,867	8	7
Rum	2,080,471 galls.	234,052	19	9
Sheep's Wool	23,677 lbs.	493	5	5
Sticks, walking ...	3,230 bundles	3,790	13	0
Succades	45 c. 1 q. 5 lbs.	81	12	0
Sugar	499,717 c. 2 q. 15 lbs.	307,826	1	3
Tamarinds	4,597 lbs.	84	16	0
Tobacco, Cigars	4,689½ lbs.	1,993	0	9
„ Manufactured ...	2,019 lbs.	155	19	0
Tortoiseshell	3,311¼ lbs.	1,572	16	10
Turtle	1,487 no.	2,323	8	9
„ prepared and dried ...	4,788⅔ lbs.	696	3	9
Wood, Bitter	314 17-20 tons	496	5	6
„ Ebony	546 14-20 tons	1,640	2	0
„ Fustic	927 15-20 tons	2,690	9	6
„ Lignum vitæ	520 19-20 tons	1,302	7	6
„ Log wood	56,605 15-20 tons	152,835	10	6
„ Mahogany	2,740 feet	32	0	0
Yam	24,021 c. 0 q. 10 lbs.	10,809	9	10

The following figures, showing the quantities and values of the principal items of produce of Jamaica exported in the years 1854, 1874, 1884, and 1885, will be interesting:—

Years	Coffee Quantity Cwt.	Coffee Value £	Cocoanuts Quantity No.	Cocoanuts Value £	Fruit, &c. Bananas Quantity Bunches	Fruit, &c. Bananas Value £	Oranges Quantity No.	Oranges Value £	Pimento Quantity Cwt.	Pimento Value £
1854	45,059	80,520	220	3	Nil	Nil	1,001,950	604	44,179	83,158
1874	92,055	336,958	1,359,895	3,710	84,771	6,358	4,796,780	3,386	51,439	36,008
1884	48,357	98,842	5,458,730	20,671	1,442,554	191,972	41,659,500	64,296	140,472	192,706
1885	80,657	157,282	6,115,872	17,906	1,417,282	129,917	22,611,390	31,660	7,447	63,867

Years	Rum Quantity Galls.	Rum Value £	Sugar Quantity Cwt.	Sugar Value £	Ginger Quantity Tons	Ginger Value £	Woods Logwood Quantity Tons	Woods Logwood Value £
1854	997,745	117,179	420,908	412,258	626	1,463	3,917	7,208
1874	1,555,114	290,267	511,182	482,779	2,434	8,260	62,403	147,564
1884	2,036,430	220,517	588,524	428,445	1,796	4,491	44,928	131,783
1885	2,040,471	234,053	499,717	307,826	928	2,690	56,605	162,836

The following table shows the imports and exports of the colony for the years 1865, 1874, and 1880, and for each year thereafter :—

YEAR		IMPORTS	EXPORTS
1865 year ended December 31	... ...	£1,050,984	£ 912,004
1874 ,, September 30	... ...	1,762,817	1,442,080
1880 ,, ,,	... ...	1,475,197	1,512,979
1881 ,, ,,	... ...	1,392,660	1,178,593
1882 ,, ,,	... ...	1,321,962	1,549,058
1883 ,, ,,	... ...	1,591,962	1,469,447
1884 ,, ,,	... ...	1,548,707	1,483,980
1885 ,, ,,	... ...	1,456,373	1,408,848

The shipping employed in the export trade of the island during the year 1885, was as follows :—

	NUMBER	TONS	CREW
Steam Vessels	370	320,371	13,360
Sailing Vessels	333	75,806	2,813
	703	396,177	16,173

The above tonnage, &c., includes the steam vessels of thirteen lines of steamers that trade with Jamaica. By nearly all of these steamships, mails are made up for all parts of the world.

The money of account in Jamaica is pounds, shillings, and pence sterling. By the present law all silver coins under the value of 6d. current in Great Britain are a legal tender in the island to the extent of 40s. in one payment, but to no greater extent (7 Vic., chap. 51) ; and all copper coins current in Great Britain are a legal tender to the extent of 12d. in one payment, but to no greater extent (6 Vic., chap. 40) ; but there is now no copper coinage current in Great Britain, and the bronze coinage which has superseded it has not been made current in Jamaica by proclamation. The other coins current in the island are Spanish and Mexican doubloons of full weight at £3. 4s.; (Columbian and other Spanish and Mexican doubloons are seldom worth more than £3 each) ; all American gold coins of $5 and upwards at the rate of £1. 0s. 6d. for $5 (one-dollar gold pieces are only current at 4s. 1d.) ; gold coins current in Great Britain and Ireland, and British silver crowns, half-crowns, florins, shillings, and sixpences, all of which are a legal tender to any extent.

By Law 49 of 1869 the issue of a nickel currency of pennies and half-pennies is authorised, and these coins are a legal tender to the extent of one shilling and of one sixpence respectively. Law 13 of 1880 authorises the issue of nickel farthings, which are a legal tender to the extent of 3*d*. in one payment.

The coins in circulation are the following :—

British coins, gold and silver, of all denominations.

		£	s.	d.
Gold doubloons (seldom seen).				
Old Mexican, average		3	4	0
Columbian .		3	0	0
Aliquot parts in proportion.				
American (United States) gold (seldom seen).				
„ Double eagle		4	2	0
„ Single		2	1	0
„ Half .		1	0	6
„ Quarter		0	10	3
„ Dollar		0	4	1
Jamaica—nickel coin : penny, halfpenny, farthing.				

IX.—Productions.

The total acreage of the island is 2,683,520 acres. Of this 270,000 acres are valueless, being in ponds, morass, rivers, rocks, and cock-pits. Of the remainder (2,413,520 acres) 596,703 acres were under cultivation and care during the year 1885, leaving 1,816,817 acres available for agricultural and pastoral purposes.

Coffee, pimento (or all-spice), ginger, and cinchona are the principal productions of the higher elevations, whilst sugar, Liberian coffee, cacao, spices, fruit, tobacco, nutmeg, cocoanuts, pine-apples, and fibre-yielding plants are grown in the lower elevations and plains. Interspersed with these are fields of guinea grass which afford abundant nutritious food for cattle and horsekind.

Sugar.—In the early days of sugar manufacture in the island the mills used for the expression of the cane were almost entirely worked by horse-power, but there are only four or five estates on which this mode of working mills still prevails, steam and water power having almost entirely superseded it. The mills on 120 estates are supplied with motive power by steam ; 40 by water ; 18 by steam and water ; and one by wind. The separation of molasses from sugar is now almost entirely effected by means of the centrifugal machine, although the old method of standing casks of sugar in tiers and allowing the molasses to gradually drain out through perforations in the casks is still followed in a few instances.

The manufacture of sugar is the principal industry of the island, but, owing to the beet-root competition, it is much reduced in price. The quantity produced during 1885 was considerably less than that produced in the previous year, owing to the cause just stated and to the drought which prevailed in almost all parts of the island during the entire year. The quantity exported was 499,717 cwt. of the value of £307,826.

In addition to the sugar exported, a large quantity (estimated at over 10,000 hhds. a year) is consumed in the island; this is principally produced by small settlers, who grow the cane on their small holdings, and extract the saccharine matter by means of a rude construction designated a "small sugar mill."

Rum.—The Jamaica Rum is the finest in the world, holding the first place in all markets for quality and merit, and commanding a higher price than the rum of any other country. The quantity exported in 1885 was 2,080,471 gallons of the value of £234,058. In addition to the rum exported about 4,000 puncheons are annually made by the large proprietors for home consumption. The small settlers do not manufacture rum from the sugar produced by them, as the working of stills of a smaller capacity than 300 gallons is under such legal restrictions as almost to be prohibited.

Coffee.—In the higher mountain districts coffee is grown which can compete successfully with that grown in any other country. The character of this coffee is indeed so well established, that notwithstanding the fluctuations in price in the plantations at lower altitudes the coffee from the higher and well-known localities (especially from the Blue Mountains) for the most part remains at the same rates, ranging from 120s. to 140s. per cwt. The exports during the year 1885 were 80,657 cwt. of the value of £157,282.

The coffee above referred to is the Arabian coffee; but Liberian coffee is being generally planted, and will soon occupy a prominent position in the produce market. The Liberian coffee is successfully grown in the plains, where labour is cheaper and more abundant than in the high mountains, and where there are no difficulties and expense in connection with transport. In addition to the coffee exported, a very large quantity is annually consumed in the island, all classes of the inhabitants being coffee-drinkers. This coffee is principally grown and cured by the small settlers, especially those living in the parish of Manchester.

Pimento.—The pimento, which is indigenous to the island, is not only a very graceful tree, but a very remunerative plant in favourable years. It grows without cultivation of any sort in ordinary pasture land, especially in the high elevations. Ever since the Crimean war of 1854 the demand for pimento in the European markets has been considerably reduced, especially in Russia, where a large quantity of this spice had been previously consumed, but under no circumstance can a pimento property become valueless to the owner. The plant grows on land left to nature, and when it comes to maturity, on the mere clearing of the ground of the bush the best of all natural grasses in the island springs up spontaneously around the pimento trees, and the pasturage, which was fruitless before, becomes of great value. The value of the pimento exported in 1885 was £38,929 less than that of the pimento exported in 1884, but this very large falling off was principally due to the total failure of the pimento crop in the parish of St. Ann owing to the drought and strong breezes.

Cinchona.—The lands on the Blue Mountain range, where the quinine-yielding trees are being cultivated, enjoy a temperature resembling that of an English May, and are, therefore, very suitable for the successful growth of the plant. This department of cultivation has not been twenty years in existence in Jamaica. It was first established under the direction of Sir J. P. Grant, and has since been developed by Mr. D. Morris, the late Director of Public Gardens and Plantations. Mr. Morris, in a recent paper, says : " Assuming that the proper elevation has been selected and that the proper kind is cultivated, the result or the profit would be that at the expense of £100 there could be put into the market 1,815 lbs. of bark, realising £363. This is the expense which would be spread over the seven years from the time of planting the tree to the removal of the bark. After the establishment of the trees—about 1,210 to the acre—the expense becomes trifling and the return annual."

There are about 5,000 acres of land now in cinchona. Of these 143 acres constitute the Government Cinchona Plantation at Belle Vue, and 2,688 acres are lands lately patented by the Government to private individuals at nominal rates for the purpose of encouraging the enterprise. The remaining acreage consists of private property, situated principally in the parishes of St. Andrew, St. Thomas, Portland, and Manchester.

Mr. Morris, in his last official report, stated that " most species of cinchona, when established in suitable soils, appear to do well in Jamaica, but evidently the most hardy and generally the most suitable for the circumstances of the ordinary planter is *cinchona officinalis,* which at elevations above 5,000 feet grows and thrives in a thoroughly satisfactory manner.

Tea.—The cultivation of this plant is now being established on some of the higher lands purchased from the Government for the purpose of cinchona planting. The results of cultivation by the Government so far have been most encouraging. A sample of *camellia thea* recently sent to England from the Government Botanic Gardens was pronounced by a firm of brokers (Messrs. George White & Company) " to be of good flavour, and to combine to a great extent the peculiar characteristics of a fine China black leaf and a Ceylon Pekoe Souchong."

Bananas.—This is the most extensive and the most valuable fruit interest in the island. The exports in 1875 were of the value of £5,590 ; in 1880, £38,556 ; in 1884, £191,972, and in 1885, £129,917. The temporary falling off in the latter year was attributable to the prolonged drought and the general depression of trade. The Director of Public Gardens, in reporting to the Government in 1884, stated that " the development of the banana industry has brought into cultivation large tracts of lands formerly lying useless or in ruinate, and it has also been the means of circulating nearly £200,000 per annum in ready money amongst all classes of the community." With ordinary care and in favourable soil the net profit of banana cultivation is stated to be about £15 per acre planted.

Oranges.—The export of oranges is increasing by rapid strides. Several well-kept plantations are springing up, which will no doubt in time yield fruit superior to any now exported ; but the trees yielding the bulk of the present export of oranges from Jamaica are self-sown seedlings, growing in cattle pastures or in the neighbourhood of coffee and provision fields, and they receive little or no cultivation. The value of the oranges exported amounts to over £30,000 per annum.

Pine-apples.—The cultivation of this valuable and luscious fruit is greatly extending. During the year 1884 a fine selection of the best English pines from Windsor Castle and Lord Carrington's nurseries was introduced into Jamaica by the Government, and the plants are now doing well. The smooth cayenne species is being introduced by the Horticultural Society. In 1880 the value of the pine-apples exported was £522 ; in 1885 it had reached £1,443.

Cocoanuts.—In a tropical country and along the sea-coast there is no tree which is at once so picturesque and so useful for shade and shelter and so valuable as a source of food for man and beast as the cocoanut. If carefully planted in favourable situations the plant will take care of itself and will cause no expense for management. An acre of land will produce 60 plants, and these will yield nuts that will realise about £10 per annum. Thus the cocoanut industry is capable of being made most lucrative. Already it has an export value of about £20,000, and a home consumption of about £10,000, so that the cocoanut industry in Jamaica is at present of an annual value of about £30,000. The thousands of acres of land bordering the sea-coast of the island are capable of immense development in this direction.

Other delicious fruits, such as the mango, the cherimoyer, the naseberry, and the sweet sop grow in great profusion without any care or cultivation ; some of these might, with care in packing, &c., become articles of export, especially to the United States, which are within a week's journey from Jamaica. The development of the fruit trade has been very rapid. In 1867 the value of the fruits exported was £728. Two years later an agency was established at Port Antonio (which was then a decaying port) for certain fruit-houses in the United States, and seven schooners were loaded with bananas. In the following year cocoanuts and oranges were added, and since then the trade has gone on progressively, and has extended itself throughout the island. Several steamers are now engaged in this profitable business, the greater part of the fruit being conveyed to New York, Philadelphia, Baltimore, and New Orleans. The following table shows the progress made in the fruit trade during the last ten years :—

ARTICLE	QUANTITY		VALUE	
	1875	1885	1875	1885
Cocoanuts, no.	2,007,893	5,115,872	£5,599 7 3	£17,905 11 0
Bananas, bnchs... ...	58,411	1,417,282	5,590 0 0	129,917 10 4
Limes, brls.	635	809¼	254 0 0	323 14 0
Mangoes, no.	57,820	166,705	43 7 4	161 5 0
Oranges, no.	4,673,820	22,614,390	3,271 13 5	31,660 2 11
Pine-apples, doz. ...	389¼	8,883	116 16 0	1,443 9 9
Shaddocks, brls. ...	6	15	0 17 6	5 6 0
Tamarinds, lbs.	4,082	4,597	204 2 0	84 16 0
			£15,080 3 6	£181,501 15 0

Cacao was an important industry in Jamaica about a hundred and fifty years ago, but it had so declined that twenty years ago the only trees in the island were a few inferior kinds scattered here and there in settlers' gardens. In 1867 the quantity exported was 133 cwt., but 10 years after it had reached 375 cwt. of the value of £1,051. Now the quantity exported is 3,028 cwt. and the value £6,360. Messrs. Lewis & Peat (English brokers), in recently reporting on samples sent them, stated that "before they named where the cacao came from it was classified as ' high class Trinidad.' "

Fibre-yielding Plants.—Increased attention is being devoted to the utilisation of the many native plants capable of yielding fibre. The most promising plants appear to be the various species of agave furcrœa, sansevieria, and the China grass or ramie (*bœhmeria nivea*). Furcrœa cubensis is widely distributed in the island and especially in the parish of Westmoreland, where it is known as "silk grass." The common keratto yields a good soap as well as a fair fibre. The bamboo is utilised also for fibre purposes, being exported in a crushed state and packed by hydraulic pressure in convenient bales. The New Zealand flax (*phormium tenax*) has been introduced, and is now established at the Cinchona Plantation.

Woods.—A large business was done in Jamaica woods to the year 1875, when the quantity exported was 85,204 tons, of the value of £265,211. Since then both the price and the quantity required have considerably fallen. During the year 1885 the quantity exported was 58,598 tons, of the value of £158,500 ; but this was larger than the exports of the previous year, which were 47,080 tons, of £140,447 value. The most valuable of the Jamaica woods are the yacca, the bullet tree, (hard almost as a bone), the mahoe, juniper cedar, Santa Maria, Spanish elm, the common cedar (from which cigar boxes and furniture are largely made), lignum vitæ, ebony, fiddle wood, yoke, prickly yellow, broad-leaf, guango, soap wood, calabash and cashaw.

Medicinal Plants.—Plants of a medicinal nature are a marked feature in the indigenous flora of Jamaica, and in works published from 1735 to the present time numerous references are made to the valuable properties possessed by Jamaica plants. Eighty-seven samples were exhibited at the New Orleans Exposition, among which was the semper vivum (*aloe vulgaris*), which grows commonly throughout the island and in the driest districts. Samples of the inspissated juice, prepared by the officers of the Botanical Department, have lately been declared in London and New York of good quality and of value as an article of commerce. Sarsaparilla is also successfully grown in the parish of St. Elizabeth and elsewhere. At the present price of sarsaparilla the gross return is estimated at 30s. per plant, or at the rate of £50 per acre. The quinine-yielding cinchona has already been noticed.

X.—PUBLIC GARDENS AND PLANTATIONS.

The Public Gardens and Plantations consist of the following :—

1. *The Botanic Gardens at Castleton.*—600 feet above sea-level, in the parish of St. Mary, 19 miles from Kingston, containing collections of tropical plants, a palmetum, experimental grounds for economic plants, and large nurseries for their successful propagation and distribution.

2. *Cinchona Plantations.*—4,500 to 6,300 feet above sea-level, on the southern slopes of the Blue Mountains, in the parish of St. Andrew, 23 miles from Kingston. About 143 acres under cinchona cultivation and 7 acres in jalap, tea, &c. Contain also nurseries for the propagation and distribution of cinchona plants and timber and shade trees for higher elevations.

3. *Hope Plantation.*—400 feet above sea-level, near the foot of the hills in Liguanea Plains, 5 miles from Kingston, containing about 150 acres, of which 15 acres are under cultivation for propagating and distributing new varieties of sugar cane; nurseries for valuable timber and shade trees; also for fruit trees, pine-apples, and plants of Liberian coffee and Trinidad cacao.

4. *Palisadoes Plantation.*—Occupying the long, narrow strip of land enclosing the Kingston Harbour, about 5 miles long; extensively planted with cocoanut palms.

5. *Kingston Parade Garden.*—A pleasure-garden and central park in Kingston; kept up with shade and ornamental trees, flowering plants, tanks, and fountains.

6. *Botanic Garden at Bath.*—The old Botanic Garden of the colony, established in 1774; still maintained as a station for the distribution of seeds and plants in the eastern portion of the island.

7. *King's House Gardens and Grounds.*—Containing about 177 acres, of which about 20 acres are kept up as an ornamental garden. Many valuable economic plants and fruit trees are also under cultivation, as well as the rarer tropical palms.

These gardens and plantations form a department of the public service and are maintained at the public cost. They are under the control of a director, who is assisted by two superintendents and four gardeners.

Plants are sold at the gardens and plantations at moderate prices. For public institutions and for persons endeavouring to promote the development of industrial products in the island, a number of valuable introduced plants are available for experimental purposes at nominal rates or free of cost. On special application to the director, plants valuable in medicine or arts, and specimens required for artistic, educational, or benevolent purposes, may be gratuitously supplied.

XI.—LANDS.

Under two local laws all lands in the possession of squatters are aken over by the Government, and all lands on which quit rents have not been paid for five years and more are forfeited to the Crown. The operations of these laws have placed the Crown in possession of over 80,000 acres of land, a large portion of which extends over the northern part of the parish of St. Thomas and the southern part of Portland. All this region consists of virgin lands, and is well-watered with numerous springs and rivers. It possesses a most salubrious climate, and ranges from 2,000 to 6,000 feet in height, and it embraces some of the finest coffee land in the island. The geological formation is chiefly of trappean and metamorphosed series, and it is of the same character as the fertile coffee lands of the parishes of St. Andrew and St. Thomas. It is rich in minerals; copper, cobalt, and lead having already been discovered in several places. The climate in the higher parts is extremely cool, and is suited to the labour of white men in the open air. European fruits have been cultivated in some of these localities, and the Government Cinchona Plantations are situated on portions of this land, which have already proved that cinchona bark can be successfully produced in Jamaica.

The lands are offered for lease and sale by the Government at the rate of 2s. an acre on the condition that "the grantee will immediately upon entering into possession commence to establish the cultivation of cinchona." If at the end of five years the grantee shall have cleared and planted efficiently with cinchona a total extent of not less than one-sixth of the land, the whole will be conveyed to him in fee-simple without further charge. A number of enterprising planters have availed themselves of these conditions, and have entered on the cultivation of cinchona, with coffee, tea, and other products suitable to the localities.

XII.—POSTAL AND TELEGRAPHIC COMMUNICATIONS.

The Post-Office Department includes the Inland Telegraph and the Foreign Money-Order Branches; the whole is under the management of the Postmaster of Jamaica, who is assisted by 17 clerks.

There are 93 District Post-Offices. The postal rates are based on a prepaid system; they are uniform throughout the island. Twopence is charged for a letter of a half-ounce; 4d. for a letter of an ounce, and 4d. for every additional ounce or fraction of an ounce. Letters for office or town delivery, or for Spanish Town, Old Harbour, Gordon Town, Cold Spring, Port Royal, Halfway-Tree, Up-Park Camp, Linstead, Ewarton, May Pen, Four Paths, and Porus are charged 1d. for the half-ounce, and 2d. for every additional ounce or fraction thereof. A post card for town or office delivery is charged 1½d., and for any distance inland 1d. Newspapers pass within the island ½d. each.

Letters for Great Britain, the Canadian Provinces, the British West India Islands, the United States of America, and all other countries that are within the Postal Union are conveyed by steamer at a uniform rate of 4d. for every half-ounce. Newspapers not exceeding 4 ounces are carried at 1d., and every additional 4 ounces or fraction of an ounce is charged 1*d.* additional. Post cards are permitted transmission at 1½*d.* per card.

There are daily mails between Kingston and Spanish Town, Old Harbour, Halfway-Tree, Gordon Town, Cold Spring, Port Royal, Up-Park Camp, Linstead, Ewarton, May Pen, Four Paths, and Porus, and tri-weekly posts between the other parts of the island.

There are 40 Telegraph Sub-Stations. The charge for telegrams throughout the island is 1*s.* for the first 20 words, and 3*d.* for every additional 5 words.

Money-orders are issued from the General Post-Office for the United Kingdom, the United States of America, Canada, British Guiana, Barbados, and Turks Islands. Money-orders for British India, Australia, South Africa, and the other principal British Colonies are paid through the General Post-Office in London. (Inland Money-orders are issued through the Public Treasury.) The Parcels-Post system is now in operation between Jamaica and Great Britain, and parcels up to 7 lbs. in weight can be sent at a postage charge of 9*d.* per lb.

XIII.—Means of Communication.

I. In Jamaica.—(1) *By railway.*—A Government railway runs from Kingston to Spanish Town, a distance of 13 miles, whence one branch goes as far as Porus, in the parish of Manchester, distant 50½ miles from Kingston, and a second branch runs to Ewarton, in St. Catherine, at the foot of Mount Diablo, distant 30¼ miles from Kingston. (2) *By carriage or on horseback.*—There are livery stables in Kingston and most of the large towns. (3) *By mail coach.*—Various lines of road are now traversed by mail coaches. (4) *Tramcars.*—These are confined to Kingston and the immediate neighbourhood. (5) *Coastal steamer.*—A steamer leaves Kingston every ten days on a trip round the island, going eastward and westward alternately, and calling at the principal ports.

II. To or from Jamaica.—(1) *Royal Mail Steam Packet Company.*—The vessels leaving Southampton (England) every alternate Thursday reach Kingston on every alternate Sunday, and vessels which leave Kingston every alternate Wednesday reach Southampton in about 17 days. (2) *West India and Pacific Steamship Company.*—Steamer leaves Liverpool for Kingston once a month on a day fixed by advertisement, calling at St. Thomas and Port-au-Prince. (3) *French Line.*—Steamers arrive at Kingston on the 13th of each month, after touching at St. Thomas, Ponce, Port-au-Prince, and Santiago de Cuba ;

E

they leave Kingston on the 16th of each month. (4) *Cunard Steamship Company.*—The steamers sail monthly from Halifax, Nova Scotia; Bermuda, Turks Islands, and Jamaica, returning by the same route a few days after their arrival in Jamaica. (5) *Atlas Steam Company.*— The steamers sail from Kingston to New York and back every fortnight; the voyage takes 6 to 8 days.

XIV.—POINTS OF TOPOGRAPHICAL INTEREST IN JAMAICA.

A stranger arriving at Kingston, Jamaica, and desirous of seeing something of the island, is often in a difficulty to find suitable information to enable him to visit points of interest without loss of time. If the visitor has only a short time at his disposal, he would be compelled to confine himself to points of interest within easy access of Kingston, and in such case could not do better than visit one or more of the following places :—

The Cantonment of Newcastle, at an elevation of from 3,800 to 4,500 feet above the sea, is about 14 miles from Kingston, of which 9 miles consist of a good carriage road to the village of Gordon Town, where ponies can be hired to ride up the beautiful valley of the Hope River. From Cold Spring Gap, above Newcastle, a view of the north-side of the island may be obtained if the fog will permit.

The next point of interest is the Bog Walk Valley, through which the Rio Cobre flows, and up which the railway to Ewarton passes. To see this valley properly, the journey should be made by the carriage road. The usual course is by rail to Spanish Town, where a carriage may be hired to proceed up the Bog Walk, at the lower entrance of which is the dam or head works of the Rio Cobre Irrigation Canal, and at the upper end is the Gibraltar Rock, through which the Ewarton Railway passes by a tunnel half-a-mile long. While passing through Spanish Town, a visit might be paid to the public buildings, including the old "King's House," the old Legislative Council Chambers, the Cathedral, &c.

Another delightful drive is over Stony Hill, down the valley of the Wag Water River, along the carriage road known as the "Annotto Bay Junction Road," to the Castleton Botanical Garden. This garden, maintained by the Government, is well worth seeing, and the scenery along the road is very beautiful. The trip to Castleton and back to Kingston is easily accomplished in one day.

If the visitor is interested in the growth of cinchona, a great portion of the mountains and much beautiful scenery may be seen by a trip to the Government Cinchona Plantation, which is on the Blue Mountain Range, about 5 miles in a straight line east of Newcastle.

A very pretty waterfall and precipitous gorge may be seen on the Cane River, 2 miles north of the little village on the Windward Road, 7 miles from Kingston.

Should the visitor have time at his disposal, and desire to take a trip round the island, we would suggest his "doing" the eastern side of the island first.

Starting from Kingston, the road is most uninteresting until you arrive near Morant Bay, in the parish of St. Thomas; from this point the country is mostly cultivated, and the scenery picturesque, with the great Blue Mountain Peak to the northward until arrival at Bath, an inland village. Here the most important object of interest is the warm bath of St. Thomas the Apostle, of which an account is given in another part of this Handbook.

An excursion into the mountains from Bath, over the bridle road known as the Cuna-Cuna Road, is most interesting. This road passes over a wild and very mountainous district, and, crossing the main ridge, enters the valley of the Rio Grande, which discharges on the north side of the island. This district will be found replete with objects of interest for the naturalist, the geologist, and the botanist.

Continuing the journey eastward from Bath for about 7½ miles, the top of Quaw Hill is reached. From this point a lovely view may be obtained of the sugar estates in the Plantain Garden River district, and the east end of the island with the lighthouse. The road hence to Port Antonio passes more or less within view of the sea, and is one of the most lovely drives in the island. Port Antonio is a pretty and thriving town, and has a fine harbour.

The road from Port Antonio to Annotto Bay crosses the beautiful Rio Grande, one of the finest rivers in the island, and passes through the villages of Hope Bay and Buff Bay, and mostly skirts the sea. There is some pretty scenery along this road, but the distant mountain scenery is particularly beautiful.

The eastern end of the island is extremely mountainous, and there are some lovely spots to be seen up the ravines and gorges of these mountains.

Should the visitor care to take a ride into the interior, we would suggest one up the Rio Grande to the Maroon village called Moore Town; and, should he care to see some of the mountain fastnesses, a walk up the Stony River to the site of old Nanny Town, although a work of great labour, will amply repay the trouble.

From Annotto Bay the main road turns inland until, at a distance of about 12 miles, the thriving seaport town of Port Maria is reached. From Port Maria the road continues through the parish of St. Mary to the White River, which is the boundary of that parish and of the adjacent parish of St. Ann. The White River Falls are very beautiful and well worth the attention of the visitor; those at Prospect are about 2 miles off the main road, and the great cascade at Cascade Pen is about 5 miles from the main road.

The main road continues through the parish of St. Ann, along the seaside to the village of Ocho Rios, which is a very pretty place. Much lovely scenery will be seen through the parish of St. Ann, and the Roaring River Falls, near the main road, 4 miles east of St. Ann's Bay, are a grand sight which no visitor to Jamaica should miss.

The town of St. Ann's Bay is prettily situated on rising ground, and is growing in importance. A trip through the parish of St. Ann will be found extremely enjoyable. We therefore suggest that the tourist should take the road from St. Ann's Bay or Ocho Rios to Moneague, where he should sleep, and starting at four o'clock on the following morning be at the top of Mount Diablo at daybreak, so as to witness one of the most extraordinary sights in Jamaica—namely, the conversion of the district of St. Thomas-in-the-Vale, which lies at the foot of the hill on the other side, into a lake of fog, which any stranger might take for water. From this spot the Ewarton Railway Station is only 5 miles distant, so the tourist may either return by rail, or, what would be better, retrace his steps to Moneague and thence follow the great interior road through St. Ann's to Brown's Town, a very pretty and thriving interior village, whence the road passes to Stewart Town, on the boundary line of the parish of Trelawny. Below Stewart Town the Rio Bueno rises—an immense body of water bursts forth in a deep pool from under a precipitous rock; this is quite a curious place, and well worth the time it will take to visit it.

The seaside road from St. Ann's Bay towards the west passes through the villages of Runaway Bay and Dry Harbour, and crosses the Rio Bueno by a fine bridge at the village of that name. Two miles to the eastward of Dry Harbour a very remarkable cave is situated near the southern side of the road. This cave is very extensive and beautiful, and the several passages underground may be traversed for a long distance; of course, a guide and candles would be necessary.

The road from Rio Bueno continues westward, through some fine sugar estates, to the village of Duncans, and thence reaches the town of Falmouth, which is a large and regularly built seaport town. The court house here is considered the finest in the island. Falmouth was once a very flourishing town, but Montego Bay, in the adjoining parish of St. James, is now its successful rival in trade.

The western districts of Trelawny, and the northern and central parts of St. James, are well cultivated, and the visitor will see some fine sugar estates. Montego Bay, the chief town of St. James, is very prettily situated, and the harbour has been much improved of late years; this place does a considerable trade. The road from Montego Bay follows the seacoast to Lucea, one of the prettiest little towns in Jamaica; the harbour is small but perfectly land-locked.

From Montego Bay the main road across the island leads to Montpelier and the "Great River," which is the boundary of St. James and Hanover. Here is a very fine bridge, after crossing which there are two roads, one going to Savanna-la-Mar, and the other to Black River. We would suggest the traveller taking the road to Savanna-la-Mar; it passes through a beautiful and well-cultivated country, and there are some very fine residences along this road. The other road to Black River also passes through some very pretty country. The chief object in taking the Savanna-la-Mar road is to see that town, and also to have an opportunity of visiting some of the fine sugar estates of Westmoreland, which is perhaps the most prolific sugar district of the island. Savanna-la-Mar is the shipping port, and a considerable amount of business is done here.

The road from Savanna-la-Mar to Black River furnishes some fine views, particularly about Bluefields. The western end of the island is rich in cultivated scenery, while that of the eastern end is wild and mountainous. At the town of Black River, the river of that name debouches, and there is a fine bridge over it near its mouth. A row up this large river to and beyond the "broad water" is worthy the attention of the tourist, particularly to one unaccustomed to the wild and tangled vegetation of its banks. The Black River is the finest river in the island; it has a tortuous course of over 40 miles, of which about 30 are navigable for good-sized boats.

From Black River the main road, which (like all the other main roads in the island) is extremely good, passes northward through Lacovia; but we would suggest the tourist taking the road through Fuller's Wood, Claremont and Pedro Plains for the purpose of visiting the "Lover's Leap," a sloping precipice 6,160 feet high, the base of which is washed by the sea. This spot is situated on the beautiful property of "Yardley Chase," where a well-conducted sanitarium is maintained. The roads from "Yardley Chase" through the Santa Cruz Mountains are good, and there is much lovely scenery. We would suggest the road past Potsdam School and northwards to the village of Santa Cruz ; here the main road is again entered ; this will lead through the beautiful pastures of Gilnock, Goshen, and Pepper to the foot of Spur Tree Hill, at the boundary of the parish of Manchester. This is, perhaps, the most trying piece of road that the visitor will have experienced in his travels, as in a distance of about 2½ miles an elevation of about 1,300 feet has to be overcome. The road, however, is a good one.

Once at the top of Spur Tree Hill, the tourist is fairly in the parish of Manchester, and, following a good road for 8½ miles farther, the picturesque village of Mandeville (so named after the son of the Duke of Manchester) is reached. This place is 2,130 feet above the sea. Here the visitor will find good accommodation, and enjoy a delicious climate, and, as the surrounding country is very beautiful, he might spend two or more days here with advantage.

From Mandeville a fine road leads to Porus at the eastern foot of the Manchester mountains. Porus is the western terminus of the railway from Kingston, whence Kingston can be reached in two and a half hours. We would, however, suggest that the visitor continue in his buggy southward to the Milk River Bath, of which an account is given elsewhere in this Handbook ; this is a most remarkable mineral spring, and the Government maintains here an establishment for the benefit of those persons needing the use of these waters.

From Milk River Bath a visit in the sugar districts of Vere will be most interesting. If the visitor is fond of adventure, a visit to the Portland Cave will amply repay him. This cave is situated at the foot of the Portland Ridge at the south-eastern extremity of the district of Vere, and is quite a curiosity ; it has many passages and may be traversed for long distances, the stalactites and stalagmites are extremely beautiful. From Vere a splendid road passing the two curious rivers called Salt River and Cockpit River leads to Old Harbour, whence there is a line of railway to Kingston, and this will complete the tour of the island to Kingston.

XV.—Provident and other Societies.

There are associations throughout the island for the aid of widows and orphans ; the granting of medical and pecuniary assistance to the respectable poor, and the relief of distress, generally. Among these may be named the Women's Self-Help Society, the Kingston Dispensary, the Charity Organisation Society, and the Jamaica Masonic Benevolence.

There are also a number of mutual aid societies in Jamaica. Among these are a Life Assurance Society, a Fire Insurance Society, seven Building Societies, a Marine Insurance Company, and a People's Discount and Deposit Company. In addition to these several institutions there are 11 branches of Foreign Life Assurance and 18 branches of Foreign Fire Insurance Societies doing business in the island.

A Government Savings Bank exists in Kingston, with branches in the several parishes. There were on September 30, 1885—15,511 individual depositors, besides the charitable societies, clubs, and public functionaries investing in their official capacities ; the amount deposited during the financial year was £223,135. The assets of the Bank on the date named amounted to £360,190. Penny Banks are also in operation in the several districts ; these are principally held at schools, and are under the management of ministers of religion and other influential gentlemen. On September 30, 1885, there were 59 Penny Banks in operation, with 13,922 depositors.

XVI.—NATURAL HISTORY OF JAMAICA.

1. BIRDS.—The number of species of birds found in the island is 189. Of this number 43 are presumed to be peculiar to Jamaica, as they are not *known* to have been found elsewhere. It is quite impossible to give the list of these birds in this small publication, but it may be found in the "Handbook of Jamaica" for 1881, pp. 103 to 117.

Space affords opportunity only of giving the common names of those birds, which, as the late Dr. Chamberlaine, by whom the list was compiled, says, "are most commonly followed by sportsmen." They are the following—the wild Guinea bird, the quail, the white-belly dove, the baldpate pigeon, the peadove, the ground dove, the mountain witch, the ring-tail pigeon (" the most luscious dainty of his class or of any other ") the blue pigeon, the white-wing pigeon, the mountain partridge, the two-penny chick, the coot, the Jamaica heron, rails, plovers, snipe, ducks of many kinds, the butter bird, sand-pipers, the pecheere, and parrots.

Gosse in his work, "A Naturalist's Sojourn in Jamaica," pays tribute to the singing birds of the island in the following graceful words :—" The groves and fields of this sunny isle ring with the melody of birds to a degree fully equal, in my judgment, to that of Europe. In the lone forests the ' glass-eye merle ' pours forth a rich and continued song; and that mysterious harmonist, the ' solitaire,' utters his sweet but solemn trills, long drawn and slow, like broken notes of a psalm, so perfectly in keeping with the deep solitude. In the woods that cover, as with an ever-verdant crown, the lower hills, the ' black strike ' and the ' cotton tree sparrow ' enunciate their clear musical calls so much alike as scarcely to be distinguished, four or five notes running up the scale so rapidly as to be fused as it were together, and suddenly falling at the end. Here too sits the ' hopping dick ' and whistles by the hour together a rich and mellow succession of wild notes, clear and flute-like, like his European cousin the black-bird. . . . But there is one master-musician, whose varied notes leave the efforts of his rivals at an immeasurable distance behind him. It is he that makes our sunny glades and shady groves eminently melodious by night and day, sustaining almost the whole burden himself. He is the nightingale of the western world, the many-voiced mocking bird. . . If all the birds of Jamaica were voiceless, except the mocking bird, the woods and groves and gardens would still be everywhere vocal with his profuse and rapturous songs."

There is a Birds' and Fish Protection Law in force in Jamaica, under which the killing of certain birds is prohibited, and a close season is prescribed for others. The sporting birds, enumerated above, are in the second class.

2. FISHES.—Almost all writers on Jamaica have united in praising the variety, abundance, and superior quality of our sea and river fish.

In "The Present State of Jamaica," by a Thomas Malthus, pub-lished in London in 1683, the following extract occurs: "There is store of fish both in the sea and divers rivers, not much common to England, but a kind of lobster, crawfish, eels, mullets, and Spanish mackarel, with abundance of all sorts of admirable fish proper to those seas. Tortoise are taken much on this coast but chiefly at the Island Caymanas, 30 leagues to the west of this island, whither the vessels go May, June, and July to load of their fish that they pickle in bulk, and take them in that season when they come on shore to lay their eggs, which they do, and cover them with sand that hatches them, and then by instinct they crawl to the sea, where they live and feed on weeds that grow to the bottom or float."

Sloane writing as quaintly says : " I knew not, neither have I heard, of any place where there are greater plenty of freshwater or seawater fishes than in the island and on the coast of Jamaica, which is a great providence and contrivance for the support of the inhabi-tants, the temperature of the climate and air hindering the salting, preserving, or drying provisions as in other countries."

Saltwater fish.—The Calipeva, or "Jamaica salmon," as it has been called from its appearance, is classed among the mullets and generally held the finest fish of the island. It ranks among three special Jamaican dainties, the other two being the ring-tail pigeon and the mountain or black crab.

June fish attain the largest size of any kind usually brought to market. The Hon. Mr. Ccke mentions one captured off Long Acre, in St. Elizabeth's parish, which weighed 314 lbs. gross, and they have been harpooned off Port Royal measuring 6 feet in length. It is regarded as excellent for the table when weighing from 10 to 20 lbs.

Grunts appear to be more common in the local market than other kinds of fish. With them are associated the croakers and drummers, all deriving their names from the singular sounds they produce.

Snappers also furnish a constant supply at all seasons, and are in good request for the table. Mutton, black, grey, and pot snappers are among the favourite varieties.

Silts constitute a very important proportion of the fisherman's harvest all round the island.

The kingfish is one of the handsomest and richest taken in these waters.

·The barracouta in its prime is by many considered equal in merit to the kingfish. It is taken at all seasons and on all parts of the coast. The name ·is spelt in various ways, but the form above is adopted from that published in the Royal Navy List as the title borne by one of Her Majesty's vessels, and most likely to be correct according to the derivation.

Freshwater fish.—The freshwater fish proper exhibit but little variety compared with those of the streams and rivers of other regions, nor are the few indigenous kinds especially abundant. The reasons probably are the precipitous and broken nature of most of the water-courses in the island, as well as the constant alterations and disturbances taking place in the channels from bad slides and floods.

Foremost amongst the freshwater fish are the two kinds of mullets— the "mountain mullet" and the "hog-nose mullet." The mountain mullet is a very delicate fish; the flesh is remarkably sweet and white, and the roe is a most *recherché* morsel. In general it is found nearly as large as the fish itself. The mountain mullet seldom exceeds 10 inches in length, and weighs half a pound, and in some instances above a pound.

The hog-nose mullet of the Rio Grande, the Swift, and Spanish Rivers, are certainly the largest and perhaps the sweetest. The head and neck are a mass of rich, sweet, gelatinous substance. The flesh has always been esteemed a dainty of no ordinary kind, and so it is. The length of the hog-nose mullet taken out of the Swift River, below the "Fish Done," will often measure 23 inches and usually weighs from 2 to 4 lbs. It is designated by this name on account of the elongation or projection of the cartilage of the upper mandible considerably over the lower, ending in a blunt point, with which contrivance it turns up mud, or the fallen leaves frequently found in conglomerated heaps, &c., in search of its ordinary food. The mandibles are supplied with strong, short teeth of a conical shape, irregularly set.

3. INSECTS.—Jamaica is singular for the great number of its insect forms and the fewness of the individual members of each species ordinarily seen. Occasionally a species will occur in great force but very locally, however, and for only a short time. It is practically almost useless to chase insects here; the nature of the country, the thickness of the vegetation, and the heat are such as to forbid it. A collector has, therefore, to keep a sharp look-out, and seize any opportunity of securing an insect which may present itself.

Beside coleoptera, lepidoptera, and hymenoptera the island is rich in species of the other orders of insects. The number of spiders is considerable, and includes some very pretty and curious examples, but, as far as is known, no attempt has been made to work them out.

It may be of interest to state that the larvæ of *Protoparce jamaicensis* is very destructive of the tobacco plant here; the larvæ of *Euthisanotia timais* not unfrequently destroy all the lilies in a garden in a few days; that of *Hyblæa puera* is common on the yoke or oak tree (*Catalpa longisiliqua*), sometimes denuding large trees of their leaves; the larvæ of *Phakellura hyalinata* attack cucumbers, often completely destroying the vines, and the larvæ of *Hymenia perspectalis* are destructive of edible calalu.

4. SHELLS.—No part of the world possesses richer conchological treasures than Jamaica, or offers more tempting prospects to the explorer for shells. The land shells are unsurpassed anywhere else for beauty and variety, and comprise no less than 221 inoperculates and 240 operculates (exclusive of numerous recognised varieties) discovered up to the present time. Not more, on the average, than one-third of the area of the shell-bearing districts has been explored as yet, and the remainder constitutes untrodden ground where splendid rewards await the collector. Several generic forms are peculiar to the island, whilst the specific forms, with the exception of about a dozen small ones, are to be found nowhere else. *Stoastoma* (except

4 species in Haiti and Porto Rico, and 1 of the subgenus *Electrina* far away in the Philippines), *Sagda* (except the subgenus *Odontosagda* in Haiti, more properly coming under *Zonites*), *Geomelania* (except 1 species of the subgenus *Blandiella* in Demerara), *Sucidella*, and *Jamaicia* belong to Jamaica exclusively. It is the metropolis of the beautiful Cyclostomas with a decollated spire and delicately frilled lip, known as *Choanopoma*, and of *Alcadia* among the Helicinidæ, with its curious slit or notched lip, and sickle-shaped or toothed columella. There is a superb collection of the land shells of Jamaica in the British Museum, presented by the late lamented Mr. Chitty, formerly one of the Judges of the island ; and a complete catalogue of the species up to this time found, arranged, however, according to the classification in the monographs of Pfeiffer, appears in the "Handbook of Jamaica" for 1883.

In these days of rapid locomotion but a few months would be taken up in a trip from Europe to Jamaica, and in going back laden with an ample collection of these lovely objects. Land shells occur in amazing numbers in the limestone districts, which constitute the greater part of the island. After becoming acquainted with their habitats, the collector may easily obtain a rich harvest of many genera and species in a single day ; while his work will be done amidst the magnificent scenery of our favoured island, and he will be securing a fresh lease of life by inhaling its refreshing and invigorating mountain breezes. If desirous of collecting the sea-shells, the collector will have but a few hours' travel to undergo in transferring himself from the interior to the seashores, which present every variety of station suited to marine species, of which nearly all those of the entire Caribbean Province are easily to be collected in Jamaica, from the littoral to no very great depths. They are of transcendent beauty, and many of them are still rare in cabinets.

It may be added that Rhizopoda, Polycystina, Spongidæ, and indeed nearly all the groups of the sub-kingdom Protozoa, are represented in great profusion in Jamaica—a single haul of the net or bag rarely fails to bring up very many new forms. Legions of the more splendid members of the Cœlenterata offer themselves to the hand of the collector. If time is left, it may be profitably employed in exploring the Bowden and Clarendon beds, which, especially the former, abound in marine Tertiary fossils still as perfect as on the day of their entombment.

5. JAMAICA STOCK.—The breeding of cattle and horses has had great attention from penkeepers, and the breed has been greatly mproved from time to time by the introduction of superior stock from England and America. At the present time our neat cattle and

thorough-bred horses will compare favourably with those of most countries, whilst they undoubtedly surpass the stock in the rest of the West Indies.

The best cattle are reared in the parishes of St. Ann, Manchester, and St. Elizabeth, the Guinea grass in those parishes being very fine and the climate well suited to the growth and development of fine stock. The fattening capabilities of the parish of St. Catherine, particularly in the Salt Pond and St. Dorothy districts, are well known. The markets of Kingston and Spanish Town are supplied with beef chiefly from cattle brought from St. Ann, Manchester, and St. Elizabeth, and fattened in St. Catherine. There are other districts in the island in which on a more limited scale neat cattle are reared, notably in St. Mary, Trelawny, Westmoreland, and Hanover, the herd of pure-bred Herefords at Knockalva in the last-named parish being the finest in the island, the six-year-old steers weighing from 1,500 to 2,000 lbs.

The horsekind in Jamaica is the finest in the West Indies. As in the case of cattle, so in that of horses, the parishes of St. Ann, Manchester, and St. Elizabeth have been found to produce the best stock. The racing stock come almost entirely from these three parishes ; and the horses of Hanover and Westmoreland are excellent and hardy stock for general use. Some of the best Jamaica racing-stock have been exported to Demerara, Barbados, Trinidad, &c., where they have always distinguished themselves. Three Jamaica race-horses have lately been exported to Mexico.

Mules are bred all over the island, but on a more extensive scale at the regular grazing farms. The mules of St. Elizabeth and Manchester are in great demand, because they are as a rule good-tempered, hardy, and cheap ; whilst the mules of Hanover, and notably those bred at Knockalva, on the borders of Westmoreland, are generally considered to be the finest in the island.

The following table shows the number of horsekind and horned cattle in Jamaica on which poll-tax was paid in the several years from 1880 to 1885, both inclusive :—

Year ending September 30, 1880	...	...	...	...	135,353
„ „ 1881	...	...	...	...	138,244
„ „ 1882	...	...	...	...	145,714
„ „ 1883	...	...	...	...	140,961
„ „ 1884	...	...	...	...	138,450
„ „ 1885	...	...	...	...	140,923

This return does not include cattle and horsekind used on estates in the island, nor animals under one year of age, as these are not subject to taxation.

6. WILD ANIMALS.—The only wild animals found on the island at its conquest by the British troops were cattle, horses, hogs, and Indian conies. Of these only hogs and Indian conies remain in a wild state. Wild hogs abound in the upper parts of the parishes of Portland and St. Thomas, and are also to be found in the backwoods of St. Ann, Trelawny, and St. Elizabeth, where they often do great damage to the provision grounds of the peasantry. Some of them grow a great size; indeed there is evidence that they have attained the height of 3 feet. The Indian cony, which is good eating, is found in rocky localities, chiefly in limestone districts. They abound in the lowlands of St. Catherine, in the St. John's mountains, in Upper Clarendon, Portland, St. Ann, and Trelawny.

In dealing with wild animals, perhaps mention should be made of the iguana and the mungoose. The iguana, which is a large lizard from 2 to 4 feet long, and much esteemed for the delicacy of its flesh, is found only on the Healthshire Hills of St. Catherine. The mungoose was introduced from India at a comparatively recent date for the purpose of destroying rats on sugar estates, and has spread all over the island.

APPENDIX.

A.—THE CLIMATE OF JAMAICA.

By DR. J. C. PHILLIPPO.

" JAMAICA," says Scoresby Jackson, a well-known English physician, " offers a great variety of climate, and is therefore one of the best of the West India Islands for invalids to reside at who can afford to move from place to place in order to put themselves in the most advantageous positions as regards their temperament and diseases. Scrofulous children and persons threatened with consumption but in whom there is no active disease might well be sent there. Persons suffering from bronchial affections, as well as persons in whom the constitution is not materially implicated, might derive benefit from a sojourn in Jamaica."

A residence of thirty years in the lowlands enables the writer to cor-roborate every word just quoted, and to state in addition that he has seen many in whom there were symptoms of active tubercular mischief who have been alleviated and even cured when due attention has been paid to the necessary hygienic laws.

Within a radius of a few miles we can obtain dry mountain situations with cheerful aspects, extensive views of tropical scenery, an invigorating stimulating atmosphere suitable to the hypochondriac and dyspeptic, and moist mountain situations for the nervous and those who suffer from a dry and irritable condition of the air-passages ; dry inland and seaside situations for the luco-phlegmatic and those who suffer from copious bronchial dis-charges, saline and sulphurous baths in the lowlands for the rheumatic and gouty, and chalybeate waters in the mountains for the anæmic.

Open-air life.—Over and beyond these advantages Jamaica permits *at all times* an open-air life, for in the mountains as well as in the plains, all the windows and doors are kept open during the day with free ventilation during the night. There are few days in the year in which open-air exercise cannot be taken in some way or other, and while we should hardly advise Europeans and Americans to sleep in the open air, our soldiers both native and European have often been placed under tents, in seasons of epidemics, with advantage.

It is the open-air life that really cures so many invalids who go to the various watering-places and summer resorts in Europe and America ; it is the open-air life that renders England's summers so beneficial to the invalid who has been shut up during the cold and dreary winter months, and we venture to affirm that an open-air life in Jamaica, with the *pure and rare atmosphere of its mountains*, will do far more for the invalid than a residence in Egypt, Syria, Mentone, Nice, or Spain for the European, or Minnesota, Nassau, or even Florida for the American.

Sea-breezes.—Jamaica being an island in the tropics is of course warm, but the hottest days and nights in the lowlands, except during the rainy seasons of April and May, September and October, are tempered by the sea and land-breezes, the former of which sets in from 10 to 11 A.M. and lasts generally until 5 to 6 P.M., and sometimes even all night, whilst the latter commences at about 8 P.M. and lasts until 6 or 7 in the morning.

Professor Parkes, in his excellent work on Hygiene, states as the result of his examination as head of the Army Medical Department of Great Britain, that for several years there were but 15½ perfectly calm days at Up-Park Camp, the Military Station near Kingston, whilst the velocity of the sea-breeze according to Mr. Maxwell Hall, the Government Meteorologist of the Island, is generally from 2 to 4 miles per hour during the winter months and from 5 to 6 in June and July.

Temperature.—Throughout the whole island the temperature is generally equable all the year round, the mean maximum in the lowlands being from 83° to 86° during the day and the mean minimum from 68° to 70° during the night. Of course there are hours when the maximum will be much higher and the minimum much lower, but rarely does the thermometer go above 90° during the winter months, and then but for a very short time, the average maximum being about 80°. The diurnal range in the lowlands is considerable, being from 15° to 16°, but as the lowest temperature is generally at about two or three in the morning, when most people are in bed, the fall is not much felt.

In the mountains the temperature varies according to altitude and exposure to the north winds, which come down pretty severely in January, February, and sometimes in December and March, but the diurnal change is by no means so great as in the lowlands. Thus at the Government Cinchona Plantation, at Bellevue, at an altitude of 4,850 feet at a distance of about 20 miles from Kingston, the daily range is not more than about 11° on an average. During the winter months, for 3 years, the mean maximum during the day was from 64° to 68° and the mean minimum at night from 53° to 57°.

Humidity.—The humidity of the atmosphere is always a matter of great importance, and in this too we can show an immense advantage over the more northern sanitary resorts, for of course the higher the temperature the less is the humidity felt. In Kingston, Professor Parkes gives the mean degree of humidity as 65° in the years 1870–73, and in 1868 it was about 77°, whilst at Boston, U.S., with a temperature of 20° it is not uncommon for the humidity to stand at 77°.

Humidity is scarcely felt in the lowlands, and fogs are never seen along the southern coast.

In the mountains the amount of humidity is very much influenced by their position, exposure, and the presence or absence of rivercourses, ravines, and ranges, particularly the latter, for while some mountain ranges attract the clouds which roll along them, as does the central range which forms the backbone of the island, there are small and lower parallel and cross ranges which do not. Some of these ranges may be very near the central or main range and yet not being directly of it, they do not attract anything like the same amount of cloud, moisture, and rain.

Rainfall.—Mr. Maxwell Hall, M.A., F.R.A.S., the Government Meteorologist, who has carefully compiled all the meteorological reports of the island for the last four years, and has had access to nearly all the meteorological reports kept by private individuals for many years before, divides the island for the registration of rainfall into four districts, stating that this distribution was observed and described by Sir Hans Sloane 200 years ago.

From Mr. Hall's observations I conclude that whilst in the southern division the rainfall during the six winter months averages somewhat above 2 inches per month, that for the west central is somewhat above 3 inches, for the northern nearly 5 inches, and for the north-eastern over 8 inches per month. The southern division is thus undoubtedly the driest, and its mountain ranges most delightful as to temperature, especially the St. Catherine, Clarendon, Manchester, and St. Elizabeth ranges.

Health resorts.—In the latter, a cross range, called the Santa Cruz Mountains, is to be found one of the driest climates in the world, at an altitude of 2,500 feet, a mean annual maximum temperature of 75·3°, and a mean annual minimum of 66·8°, with but 38·25 inches of rain for the whole year. In this district and in a similar district in the northern division called the Dry Harbour Mountains of St. Ann, the soil is dry, with a porous limestone beneath, through which the rainfall quickly percolates; the air is simply delicious, and the driving roads are excellent.

According to Dr. Clark, of Santa Cruz, the climate is very similar to that of Algiers plus the altitude. Rarely do Europeans suffer from disease of any kind in our mountains; they are a perfect Paradise for children, and frequently do those who live in the lowlands regain in them the strength, elasticity, and tone of which a long residence in the invariable, rather than the excessive, heat of the plains has deprived them. Dr. Robb, the Principal of the Presbyterian College in Kingston, in an article on the Climate of Jamaica in the Handbook for 1883, gives, as an instance of European longevity, the fact that on one day, in the mountains of St. Ann, eight men met, most of whom were English and Scotch, of whom none had been a shorter time in the island than 43 years, most of them 50, and whose united ages amounted to 579 years ; and Dr. Clarke, of St. Elizabeth, in an article on the same subject in the Handbook for 1884, says that during a residence of 14 years in the Santa Cruz Mountains no death from fever had occurred in his practice, and that on one occasion he had on his visiting list 7 Europeans and 2 natives whose ages added together amounted to 751 years.

F

Instances of this kind can be multiplied indefinitely, and are known to almost everyone who has lived for any time in the country as occurring not only in the mountains but also in the lowlands. Here old age finds a kindly equable climate and flourishes accordingly, and, strange to say, it forms one of the largest items in our bills of mortality.

Rate of mortality in Jamaica.—A general registration has only been kept for the last 5 years, and we cannot therefore give any longer record, but the following results as published by the Registrar-General gives a pretty fair idea of the normal state, the years 1879–80 and 1880–81 being whooping-cough years—seasons of epidemic:—

1878–79	mortality per 1,000		23·9
1879–80	,,	,,	27·0
1880–81	,,	,,	26·0
1881–82	,,	,,	20·0
1882–83	,,	,,	23·0

giving an average of 23·9 per 1,000 of population.

Of course some places are more healthy than others, and, strange to say, the much-maligned Port Royal shows, according to Dr. Scott, late Officer of Health of the parish, a mortality from all diseases in the whole town, leaving out those who came from abroad ill with fever and died in the Naval Hospital in—

1881	per 1,000 of population		15·1
1882	,,	,,	16·3
1883	,,	,,	19·1

an average of 16·8, by no means large compared with many of the seaports in more northern countries.

Invalids and others who seek Jamaica in order to escape the ills of winter, are often doubtful whether in attempting to escape Scylla, they may not fall into Charybdis; whether in point of fact the diseases indigenous to the climate may not prove more fatal than those which they desire to avoid, alleviate, or cure. Precautions are necessary in every climate, and if those which are taken elsewhere by those whose vital powers are below par are taken in Jamaica, there is no fear that they will get those fevers which have been so fatal in past times, in the West Indian tropics, and which still occasionally crop up, though no longer in the severe epidemic form which characterised them then, and which they still exhibit in other countries.

It cannot be denied that fevers do arise spontaneously in certain localities amongst unacclimatised Europeans who have most probably exposed themselves to several and generally to the whole of the following conditions—viz. exposure to the midday heat, wet clothes, wet feet, fatigue, exposure at night to the chills and malaria arising from lagoons and swamps after sunset, and, above all, intemperance in drink. Let him avoid these conditions, and the European will avoid fatal fevers.

In Jamaica there are no large cities with large immigrant populations crowded together in lodging-houses, lanes, courts, and alleys, as in Buenos Ayres, Rio de Janeiro, Peru, Cuba, and other states and cities of America;

and our soldiers are no longer crowded together in ill-ventilated barracks as in former days, so that disease does not get infective strength from condensation.

Numbers of travellers have been through the length and breadth of the island, who, by a simple obedience to the advice of old residents and attention to those hygienic rules which they would follow as travellers in other lands, have not only been free from illness of any kind, but have returned to their homes strengthened and improved in health; in spite of all the inconveniences that have to be borne in a country where travellers are few comparatively, the population scarce, scattered, and poor, and travelling accommodation in consequence comparatively destitute of those conveniences and luxuries which travellers consider necessary in these days.

Next in importance to the presence or absence of fevers fatal to Europeans in the island, comes the question as to the presence or absence of the disease which in Europe and America is even more fatal and more widespread than these—namely, tubercular diseases and more particularly phthisis or consumption. This disease is here, as elsewhere, one of the most fatal and most common. People born in the most favoured climates are not exempt from it. " Even the inhabitants of Nice," says Jourdannet, himself a Frenchman, " are not free from pulmonary tubercle. Phthisis is not rare on the shores of the Mediterranean, but let an individual come to these favoured spots, from the rigorous climate endured for a long time, and he will find all his functions at ease in the midst of a milder temperature."

Jamaica as a resort for invalids.—Instances abound in this country of persons who have come from Europe and America, who have found relief and health even in the lowlands, and to a greater extent in the mountains; and the development of the disease has been arrested in the persons of their children and their children's children.

Owing to the fact that there is but about one qualified medical man out of Kingston to 10,000 or 11,000 of the population, and that the people are scattered throughout the island, far away from medical men, and as a body unable to avail themselves of their services, from 80 to 86 per cent. of the registered deaths are not authoritatively certified, and the registers are therefore doubtless very erroneous as to the real causes of death when the diseases are complicated or unknown to the informants.

Consumption, however, is by no means unknown to the unscientific, and less error is likely to be made about it than other diseases.

All diseases, however, of the respiratory organs of a chronic character are generally called consumption or decline, and chronic diarrhœa from whatever cause is associated with it as " *downward decline.*"

We may therefore conclude that the Registrar's entry of phthisis or consumption rather errs on the side of excess than otherwise.

For the last 5 years the number of deaths from this disease has amounted to between 1,000 and 1,100 in a population of 600,000 averaging about 1·59 deaths per 1,000, whilst the average of 10 years in Ireland was

1·8, in England 2·2, and in Scotland, 2·8. The average to the total number of deaths being 7 per cent. in Jamaica, 10·2 per cent. in England, 11·1 per cent. in Ireland, 12·2 in Scotland, and 10 to 11 per cent. in Canada.

The mortality from phthisis varies in various districts in this as in other countries.

Thus in the last-named country the average to the total mortality is 3·7 per cent. as the lowest and 17 per cent. as the highest.

Here in the parish of St. Elizabeth, which comprises a large area of lowland and swamp, as well as the far-famed Santa Cruz Mountains, it amounts to ·86 per 1,000 per annum, and on its mountains about *nil*, whilst in the parishes, all of them partly lowland and partly mountain, it rises until it reaches to 8·9 per 1,000 in Kingston. This, however, is partly due to the fact that, being the chief city as well as parish, it is resorted to by many who seek for domestic service, because they are unfit for field labour, and are suffering from the disease in its incipient stages or are in search of cure. That this disease is not increasing is shown by the fact that the Registrar's returns show a steady proportion of 1·9 per 1,000 of the population during the last 5 years, and that according to the observations of Dr. Lampriere, of the Army Medical Staff, who resided in Spanish Town, in the plains of St. Catherine in 1795 and 1796, it amounted to 2·88 and 2·78 per 1,000, whilst during the last 5 years it has been on an average 2·1 in the same district.

These statistics show no immunity from phthisis amongst our population; but when it is remembered that there are but about 14,000 of unmixed European descent, and that these are for the most part in comfortable circumstances so far as food, raiment, and lodging are concerned, whilst the native negro population generally live under less fortunate circumstances, it can be readily understood in which class· the mortality from phthisis is greatest, and how small the percentage must be amongst those from more northern climes who have made this island their home. The mortality among the black troops is about 8 to 1 of the white. Whilst we can thus hold out inducements to persons suffering from bronchial and incipient tubercular diseases to make our island a temporary and even a permanent place of residence, we by no means lack inducements for those who suffer from gout and rheumatism. The mere fact of the equability of our temperature is sufficient to show how desirable a climate it is for those who are compelled during the long winter months to be shut up in close and heated rooms. Gout and rheumatism are by no means rare even here amongst our natives, but, as it has been said before, with regard to other diseases, the change from a more rigorous climate has a wonderful effect on the stranger. Here, at all events, the gouty and rheumatic can enjoy the fresh air, and we can offer him, in addition, medicinal baths which have, even on our seasoned natives, and still more on visitors from Europe, the West India Islands, Honduras, and all the Central American States, a most beneficial effect.

Many who have visited us as cripples have left us cured, at all events for a time, of their infirmities, and most grateful to our little island for the benefits derived from her medicinal springs.

Jamaica is famed for its springs. Its very name is derived from the old Indian word for " *the Land of Springs*," and not a few of them are more or less medicinal.

Of these, however, but a few are in any request; the principal being a sulphurous sodic-calcic thermal, at the Village of Bath; a saline calcic thermal, at Milk River, in Vere; a cold saline calcic, at Port Henderson, near Kingston; a strong chloro-calcic, in St. Ann's; and an acidulous ferro-aluminous, in the mountains of St. Andrew.

The mineral springs of Jamaica.—1. The Bath of St. Thomas the Apostle is situated near the village of Bath, in the parish of St. Thomas some 20 miles from Kingston by a good driving road, but reached more easily by the coasting steamer, which lands passengers some 8 or 10 miles from it. There is no hotel in the village, but board and lodgings are to be obtained at a small cost in clean and comfortable cottages. It is rather a pretty West Indian village, the cottages being all of two storeys, on one side of the main road, which is bordered on each side by an avenue of Otaheite-apple, breadfruit, and mountain cabbage trees. Though not more than 170 feet above the level of the sea, the air is pure and pleasant in certain seasons of the year, but, as the district lies below the Blue Mountains, it is more than usually humid and rainy. It should therefore be visited by invalids only during the months of February, March, April, June, and August, as then there is no chance of getting a wetting in going to and from the springs. They are also in these months hotter, and contain a larger amount of their mineral constituents.

The bath-house is about 1½ mile from the village, and is reached by a pretty-good driving road, which passes through a narrow gorge to a deep ravine in which the springs rise.

These, some cold and some steaming, run across the road beyond the bath into the Sulphur River below. The house is in good order, having two large sitting-rooms, plainly furnished, in the upper storey, for the accommodation of visitors, and five bath-rooms on the ground floor, each containing a plunge bath, two of marble for ladies, and three for gentlemen.

Into these baths the water from the hot springs is led by means of a stone gutter, the hottest water coming from the *kettle* at a temperature of 182° Fahr. The *kettle* is so called because it is covered in by stonework, and has an iron lid at its apex, which when lifted gives exit to a considerable volume of steam.

The springs may be ranked among the *hot sulphuro-sodic-calcic waters*, and in some respects resemble those of Bath in England, and the Salt Lake springs in Utah, but are more closely allied to the Eaux Bonnes and Eaux Chaudes in the Pyrenees, of which Pidoux, the eminent physician and balneologist, states in his work on phthisis "that by the rare combination in them of the sulphites of lime and soda they furnish the most beautiful problem in therapeutics, the most powerful remedy in phthisis."

Be this as it may, there can be no doubt of the value of this class of waters in various diseases, and these, according to Dr. Sibly, for many years physician to the bath, " *are almost magical.*" They are stimulant and highly beneficial in many chronic complaints, and a great variety of skin diseases, *chronic rheumatism and gout*, amenorrhœa, and chlorosis, syphilitic diseases of all kinds, and diseases of the spleen and liver caused by malaria. Long, who wrote a history of the island in 1774, describes it as "sending a thrilling glow through the whole body," and states that "its continued use enlivens the spirits, and sometimes produces almost the same joyous effects as inebriation, on which account some notorious topers have quitted their claret for a while, and come to the springs merely for the sake of a little variety in their practice of debauch, and enjoy the singular felicity of getting drunk with water."

Bath was the resort of the gay and wealthy in those days, who had neither the desire nor opportunity of reaching Europe by the slow trading ships, but is now only visited by those who require its healing waters or desire to see it from curiosity. According to Professor Turner, who analysed this water many years ago under considerable disadvantages, as it was sent him in a bottle closed by an ordinary cork, one pint contains—

Carbonate of soda	...			·21 gr.
Chloride of sodium	...		...	1·48
Chloride of potassium	...		...	·04
Sulphate of soda	...	...	...	·79
Sulphate of calcium	...	...	...	·62
Silicate of soda	...	...	...	·45

Organic matter, baregine and glairine, undetermined, sulphuretted hydrogen undetermined, and almost identical results were arrived at by the island Chemist, Mr. Bowrey, a year or two ago.

2. Milk River Bath is situated in the parish of Clarendon, near the sea-coast and on the banks of the Milk River, which is navigable by small vessels only. It can be reached by the coasting steamer from Kingston which makes the trip in a few hours, or by a land journey of 30 miles by rail and 7 by driving road.

There is no hotel at the bath, but there are several houses near the springs, which are kept in good order and tolerably well furnished and provided with beds, clean bed and table linen, cook and butlers, by the Government under an old arrangement with the donor of the spring, at the small charge to visitors of 1s. 6d. per diem each, leaving them to provide for themselves or to make arrangements with the matron, who will supply breakfast, dinner, and tea for $1 to $1½ per diem.

The invalid should avoid the rainy months of October, November, and December, and the mosquito months of May, June, and July ; and would do well to provide himself with a hired vehicle so as to move about at his will, and obtain such extra supplies as he may require from the neighbouring village, where there is a Post-Office and Telegraph Station.

The mineral spring at Milk River Bath is a saline calcic thermal with a temperature of 92°, and is very similar in its constituents and its effects to the warm springs of Madison County, North Carolina, and is stronger and hotter than the Lebanon springs of New York and the healing springs of Bath County, Virginia, all of which are highly esteemed in the United States.

Instances are innumerable of the cures effected by it of sufferers from gout and rheumatism from all parts of the island, as well as from England, the United States, and Canada, the neighbouring islands, and the Spanish Main. Many who have been carried into it have after three or four baths been able to walk about by themselves, and others have left their crutches behind them for the benefit of new comers.

Some of these have gone so far as to rank it superior to the thermal saline waters of Hamburg, Wiesbaden, Kissingen, and Bourbonne from their own practical experience so far as gout is concerned; and there is no doubt but that some alteration in the structure of the bath and evaporation of the water would even give it some of the valuable action of the Kreuznach Waters so much recommended by Scanzoni for scrofula, glandular disorders, and uterine tumours. The analysis published by the Directors as furnished them lately by Savory and Moore, of London, gives the following mineral constituents in one pint of water :—

Chloride of potassium	...	...	1·44
Chloride of magnesium	...	...	37·08
Chloride of sodium		...	186·93
Chloride of calcium	...	...	13·50
Sulphate of soda	...	...	...	27·80

besides traces of lithia, bromine, and silica; an amount of mineral constituents far superior to the waters of Schlangenbad, in Nassau, and the King's Bath of Bath, in England.

8. The Jamaica Spa, consisting of two *accidulo ferro-aluminous* springs, is situated in the mountains some 4 hours by driving and riding roads from Kingston at an altitude of about 8,000 feet. The springs belong to Government, and were many years ago in great request; but the buildings have been allowed to decay, and lodgings are scarce, so that they are very little known though they are of great value and interest.

Unlike the chalybeate springs of Europe, they contain a great deal of alum, in which peculiar property they resemble the alum springs of Virginia, while they contain a much larger amount of iron than most of them.

One pint of this water contains four times as much iron as St. Moritz, in the Engadine and Schwalbach, more than twice as much as any of the springs of the Spa in Belgium, as much Epsom salts as Pyrmont, and 300 times as much alum as Pyrmont and St. Moritz; Spa and Schwalbach having none.

It is cool and colourless, but leaves a red deposit on standing for a time in the glass; is not at all disagreeable, being rather sharp, giving an astringent sensation to the gums, the iron and saline constituents being distinguished after taking the glass from the lips rather than during the process of drinking.

The following analysis, made by Professor Turner many years ago, gives the mineral constituents in one pint of water :—

Carbonate of lime	...	...	...	·868
Sulphate of magnesia	...	...	...	2·831
Sulphate of iron	...	...	...	2·21
Sulphate of alum	...	...	...	4·168
Organic matter	...	...	...	Undetermined

a combination of qualities which render it invaluable in anæmia chlorosis, amenorrhœa glandular diseases, and all the diseases caused by malaria and exhaustion.

B.—JAMAICA AS A WINTER RESIDENCE FOR NORTHERN PEOPLE.

By G. E. HOSKINSON, Esq., late Consul for the United States of America.

So many letters are received at the Consulate from people in the United States making inquiries as to the climate, character, and cost of living in Jamaica, that I very willingly take the opportunity offered me by the compilers of this Handbook to briefly outline some of the points which would be likely to interest those seeking a refuge from the wintry blasts of the North.

Climate.—The climate is mild in the winter months—soft, relaxing, and perhaps enervating to people directly from the North. The tourist coming to this beautiful island with his mind attuned to meet nature in her kindliest mood falls under the spell ; he loses interest in those things which seemed of absorbing importance at home, and is content to drink in the sunshine, and inhale the soft, balmy breezes of the tradewinds with hardly a thought of the flight of time. Days, weeks, months flee away—'tis the land of Circe— nothing changes—life flows on like a gentle stream—and surrounded by a generous and hospitable people, the stranger soon comes to lose the feeling of strangeness, and becomes as one to the manner born. One day is as like to another as it well can be. The range of the thermometer in January is from 71° Fahr. to 85°, the mean being 75° : February 70° to 86°, mean 75° ; March 71° to 84°, mean 75° ; the mean of December is about the same ; of November about 76°. In January the thermometer usually ranges as follows : 7 A.M., 71·3° ; at 3 P.M., 82·8° ; at 11 P.M., 72·8° ; at 4 A.M. 69·8°. During these months a strong sea-breeze, the regular trades, sets in about 8 A.M. and continues steadily from the south-east until nearly sunset. It tempers the heat very considerably, and is gratefully termed by the inhabitants "The Doctor." The nights are rendered pleasant and agreeable by the land-breeze from the opposite direction. The wet season usually begins in May and continues throughout that month and June and along into July. Then we have frequent showers until the month of October, when the wet season begins again, and continues until about the middle of December.

Then we have very dry weather until May. I am speaking now of Kingston. There are no malignant or contagious fevers or epidemics of any sort here, the popular idea that this is a " fever stricken hole " being entirely erroneous. For people of temperate habits Jamaica is as healthy a place for residence as any in the United States, and in this, I think, the records of the Medical Bureau will bear me out.

THE COST OF LIVING.

Generally speaking I do not think it more expensive than in New York. At the well-known hotel where I am staying, Parke Lodge, the charge for board of transient guests is 10s. 6d. or $2·50 per day. This includes everything, early coffee at 7 A.M., breakfast at 9.30, luncheon at 2 P.M., tea at 5 P.M., and dinner at 7 P.M. ; clean, airy, and well-furnished rooms, lights, baths, attendance, boots, &c. Permanent boarders pay $10·50 per week. Myrtle Bank is a very pleasantly situated seaside hotel, admirably equipped, and is also a very popular resort. Same charges as Parke Lodge. There are also many excellent lodging-houses where small parties could make themselves comfortable at rather less rates than those named above.

HOUSE RENT.

A furnished cottage, containing three bedrooms, small drawing-room, piazza, dining-room, and the necessary servants' out-rooms, could be rented at from £8 to £9. 10s. per month, free of all taxes. An unfurnished cottage, in a pleasant neighbourhood, might be obtained at about £5 per month. A small "pen," in the neighbourhood of Half-way Tree, say of 5 or 6 acres of ground, with a good residence, embowered amidst trees and shrubbery, might be rented at about £10 per month. Inquiries for houses should be made in advance, either through the Consulate, or of some of the house agents in the city, of whom I may mention, as thoroughly responsible, Messrs. Turnbull, Mudon, & Co. ; Messrs. Alexander Berry & Son ; Mr. Jos. Stines.

SERVANTS' WAGES.

Servants' wages are moderate enough, but more servants are required to do household work than in the Northern States. The chief personage in the *ménage*, the cook, receives 8s. per week, and is supposed, a popular fiction, I am afraid, to provide her own food; the butler receives 6s. to 8s. ; the house-cleaner, 6s. ; laundress, 6s. ; boy, 4s. to 6s. ; and the coachman, if you keep a " trap," 6s. to 8s. The food supplies are purchased from day to day, as they are wanted—the cook going to the market every morning. The boy goes for the ice and the morning newspapers. Servants sleep away from the premises where they are employed, as a rule, and find their own food out of their wages. At least, they are supposed to do so, but I fancy they manage somehow to exist without spending much money on food supplies.

THE MARKETS.

Kingston has an excellent market, which is always abundantly supplied. The slaughterhouse, where all the animals for the market are killed, is under strict Government supervision, and the quality of the meats exposed for sale is good. Beef, roasts and steaks, 6d. to 7½d. (12 to 15 cents) per pound; mutton, 1s. per pound (25 cents); fowls, 2s. to 2s. 6d. each (50 to 75 cents) according to weight; fresh fish, 6d. per pound (12 cents). Vegetables are cheap and plentiful. Fruits are offered in profusion, and are always cheap. I think every species of tropical fruit is grown here. Bread is delivered every morning at the door, in bakers' carts, and is of excellent quality, and, considering the heavy duty on flour, surprisingly cheap. The threepenny loaf is about the same size and weight as the five cent loaf at home. The grocers' shops are well supplied with every description of canned goods at reasonable prices. Wines and spirits are of good quality, and cheaper in price than in New York. A good table claret costs about 2s. the quart; sherry, 3s.; port, 4s. to 5s,; champagne, 6s. to 8s., the latter for "Monopole." Three star brandy, 6s.; best Scotch or Irish whiskey, 4s. Fuel is supplied in small bundles of sticks from the woodcutters' carts. Charcoal is very generally employed in cooking. They are, either of them, cheap enough, and very little of either is required. It is surprising what a good old cook will effect with a Dutch stove and a handful of coal, and what marvel of the culinary art will emerge from their smoky dens, where you can see nothing but what looks like a blacksmith's shop—a high brick bench and a huge chimney.

How to reach Jamaica.

At present there is but one line of passenger ships running between New York and Jamaica—the Atlas Steamship Company. The office of the Company in New York is at 21 and 22 State Street. The ships of this line are staunch and seaworthy, the passenger accommodations are good, the attendance good, and the table abundantly supplied. The commanders are thorough seamen, and, without exception, are respected and esteemed by all who sail with them. No lady need hesitate to entrust herself and her children to their care. The voyage usually occupies six to six and a half days. The fare is $50 either way.

The Best Time to come to Jamaica.

It has been asked if the latter part of November is too early in the season for Northern people to arrive in Jamaica. I think not. There will be more or less rain in November, but it does not interfere with freedom of movement. Sudden and heavy showers will fall—of brief duration, however—then the skies will as suddenly brighten again, and in half-an-hour's time there will be no trace of the late rain. The town is built upon ground rising up gradually from the sea, and the water soon runs off. Street-cars traverse the main streets, so that getting about is easy at all times. In addition, there are always light-running buggies on the street, called "busses," which carry the single passenger to any point within the city limits for 6d.

For Consumptives.

I do not know of any place in the world where weak lungs stand so good a chance of improving as in Kingston. The climate is so dry that damp clothing—hung up in a room—soon throws off all moisture, and the range of the thermometer so even that one, practically, may live in the open air throwing open doors and windows and permitting a free movement of air day and night. Perhaps these lines may meet the eye of someone in the early stages of phthisis; if so, I earnestly recommend the sufferer, if possible, to arrange for a few months' life in Kingston. On arrival do not be persuaded to try " the hills," as being cooler ; this dry, even climate is what is needed to effect an improvement in health.

THE SCENERY OF JAMAICA.

Having thus briefly sketched some of the practical incidents of a winter residence in Jamaica, I might well pause here, and leave to other hands the pleasing labour of dwelling upon the scenery of Jamaica and the character of the Jamaica people. Yet, having said so much, I feel that something is also due from me to the people of Jamaica, who, for over 10 years, have been uniformly kind and courteous to me and mine.

Almost any climate, or any moderate degree of temperature, may be obtained here by advancing from the seacoast up into the mountains. Within 9 miles of Kingston you can reach, with a carriage, in little over an hour's drive, the pretty little mountain village, Gordon Town, about 1,000 feet above the sea. Here the days are bright and warm, the air fresh and invigorating, and the nights cool and sleep-invoking. The Santa Cruz Mountains are highly recommended for those who need a dry, crisp, and exhilarating climate. The main drawback is the fatigue of reaching these desirable situations in the mountains, though the facilities for travel have been greatly increased of late years.

There is a coasting steamer making the circuit of the island every ten days, the time being taken up in coming to anchor every night and stopping to land and receive passengers and cargo at every port. The Government Railway extends from Kingston to Porus, distant 50 miles. Mail coaches connect with the railway at Porus for Mandeville, 10 miles. You take the 8.10 A.M. train at Kingston for Porus, there at 10.80 A.M. you take the coach for Mandeville, which place you reach, after a toilsome ascent of 2,200 feet, about noon, and with an appetite sharpened by the journey and the mountain air, will be prepared to do ample justice to the capital luncheon set out for you by mine hostess of the Brooks' Hotel.

Again, you take the 8.10 A.M. train for Spanish Town, and at 9 A.M.* an easy coach, with three mules abreast, receives you and whisks you through the solemn and almost deserted old town, a mournful spectacle of untimely decayed greatness ; through the Bog Walk (corruption for Bocco del Aqua), a picturesque gorge in the St. Catherine Mountains, through which the Rio Cobre makes its turbulent way to the sea, across the plain, or valley rather, of St. Thomas-ye-Vale ; over Mount Diablo, a passage never to be forgotten for the grandeur of its scenery ; across the rolling table-lands of the district of St. Ann's, whose green pastures and herds of fat cattle grazing upon a thousand hills will form a picture of rural peace, of charming, pastoral, out-door life that will haunt the memory of the sightseer for many a future day,

---

* Since the above was written, and just before the publication of the Handbook, the Railway Extension to Ewarton, at the foot of Monte Diablo, was opened.

and in the cool of the evening you will be set down in old St. Ann's Bay, where Columbus once spent a weary six months in pain and suffering and hope deferred, and, if you are as fortunate as I have been, some hospitable friend, all smiles and cordiality, will be waiting to receive you, and tender you a true Jamaican welcome.

For beauty and variety of scenery nothing more lovely, or grand, or magnificent could be desired than Jamaica affords. Nature here is in her holiday attire the year round ; the hills are clothed with verdure to their summits, and sparkling streams make their brawling way down the mountain sides in every direction to the sea. The people are kindly and hospitable to a degree, and they have so fine a courtesy in extending their hospitality that it almost deludes the stranger into the belief—a belief they endeavour to impress—that he is really doing them a favour in accepting it. A letter of introduction to one family in Jamaica will be a passport to several others. And this is of the greatest consequence in a social way. I have known some very pleasant people who have come out here from the United States to spend the winter who have confessed to me that they had lost a great share of the pleasure they might otherwise have enjoyed had they taken the pains to supply themselves with a few letters of introduction. Finally, a contented and philosophic spirit is a large ingredient in the enjoyment of a winter in the tropics. Americans are very like the English : whatever is different from that they are accustomed to is quite likely to be, in their opinion, mean and inferior. This does not always follow, but the constant expression of the sentiment is certain to breed a corresponding feeling toward the stranger.

C.—JAMAICA AS A HEALTH RESORT, AND AS A PLACE TO SETTLE IN.

By the Rev. ALEXANDER ROBB, M.A., D.D., Principal of the Presbyterian College, Kingston, Jamaica.

I.—Jamaica as a Health Resort.

There lies before the writer a list of 8 men, who met one day in St. Ann's in 1855. One of them wrote it on the spot, and handed it the writer of this the same day, with the heading : "Who says that Jamaica is unhealthy ?" Three of them were white Creoles, aged 86, 79, 71. The rest were English and Scotch, and only 2 of them were under 70. None of them had been a shorter time in the island than 48 years ; most of them had been 50. Their united ages amounted to 579 years. Before they died the amount would have exceeded 600.

The climate of Jamaica, which favours in men of sobriety a longevity so marked, undoubtedly offers to persons suffering from certain maladies, common in colder regions, unique advantages in stemming their ravages and prolonging life.

Rising to 7,000 feet above the sea, and lying between 17° and 19° of north latitude, Jamaica has a considerable range of temperature. Being only 160 miles long, and 40 broad, and situated in the track of the trade-winds, a most healthful sea-breeze blows over its length and breadth, during the day, with great constancy, the greater part of the year. At night a cool and gentle land wind breathes down from the mountains.

At 225 feet above the sea, near Kingston, the mean yearly temperature is 78°; and at 3,800 it is but 60°. All these circumstances secure a peculiarly favourable climate. Moderated by the sea-breeze the heat is endurable even at the sea-level, while at the higher levels the cold is not too great for even the tenderest throats and chests. In his valuable treatise on the climate of Jamaica,* Dr. Phillippo emphasises this fact, that even delicate invalids can live virtually in the open air; for, provided they are protected from direct currents, doors and windows may be left open day and night without the slightest danger. And this life in the free, open, pure air is one of the best means of preserving health, and of restoring it when it is impaired.

Unhealthy spots are chiefly those near lagoons, but they are of very limited extent, and cannot lessen the general salubrity.

A priori, therefore, it might be expected that for persons suffering from weak or affected lungs, with a tendency to bronchial and tubercular disease, there is in Jamaica the most favourable climate possible. And this, *à priori* is established as fact beyond question by the extensive experience of people of all classes. There are few of us but can tell of those we have known, seriously threatened and in danger, taking refuge here, with speedy and with much advantage. Persons who could scarcely have hoped to live through a northern winter, by coming hither have been so far restored as to live for years, and accomplish much important work. A near relative of the writer was sent here from Dublin to escape the winter of 1866. He had a threatening bronchial affection, the result of a neglected cold, and his medical adviser considered this the only probable way to prolong his life. After some months' residence in this island, he was able to undertake the inspectorship of the foreign risks of a large British insurance company; and in the discharge of his duties he visited the chief ports of South America on the Atlantic and Pacific coasts, the chief of the West India Islands, the chief ports of India, China, and Japan, besides other places, chiefly in the tropics, surveying, preparing, and transmitting elaborate reports during a period of 6 years. Some, of course, we know to have come in vain, having died here, or on the way home, or after their arrival there. Others, after residing here for a longer or a shorter period, have returned to Europe and lived and laboured for many years.

In fact, the experience is so extensive, and its testimony so assuring, that we may hold it settled, that persons of the class mentioned who can come to Jamaica may do so with the best of hopes.

And these results of general experience are corroborated by the unanimous testimony of medical men. Jamaica meets the *beau ideal* of Sir John Richardson, the eminent physician, who wrote, as quoted by Dr. Phillippo,

* " The Climate of Jamaica," by James Cecil Phillippo, M.D., L.R.C.S. (Edin.) &c., London, T. and A. Churchill, 1876. A new edition is in preparation.

in the fifth chapter of the above work, which supplies most important information on this subject: "A hypothetical consumptive Atlantis should be near the seacoast; sheltered from north winds; with a dry soil, and pure drinking water; and a mean temperature of 60°, with an average of not more than 10° or 15° on either side." Such an Atlantis can be found at more than one place in this island.

The late L. Q. Bowerbank, M.D., F.R.C.P. (Edin.), than whom there is no more honest or competent witness, wrote : " There can be no doubt that where a predisposition to tubercular or scrofulous disease exists, a residence in Jamaica will completely check its further development ; and even during the earlier stages of tubercular consumption, if its progress be not arrested, life is often prolonged, and the disease divested of much of its suffering." This is quoted from a Paper by Logan D. H. Russell, M.D., &c., published by Unwin Brothers, London, 1879, which Paper is partly also the production of Robert Russell, B.L. (Jamaica), &c., and contains much information, interesting and valuable to those who may be looking out for a place of settlement abroad. Dr. Russell (p. 5) makes a statement which, if proved correct, is of special value to those in whom tubercular disease is more advanced, and who have less to hope from a residence in Kingston or near the sea-level. It is that residence at the higher altitudes, as, for instance, at Newcastle, 4,000 feet above the sea, will probably confer special advantages, and give fair hopes of recovery, even " though softening and disintegration of the pulmonary tissue be in progress." A buoyancy of spirit, elasticity of frame, a perceptible diminution of expectoration, and an early cessation of cough, with entire absence of night perspirations, appear to be the advantages obtainable by those suffering from phthisis who will for a residence seek altitude.

The very great advantages offered by Jamaica to such sufferers are thus manifest. Within a comparatively small compass any variety of temperature and of elevation that may be best for the invalid can be obtained.

A second class of invalids to whom Jamaica offers special advantages is that of those who suffer from gout, rheumatism, and calcareous affections (Dr. Russell, ib., and Dr. Phillippo, "Climate of Jamaica," p. 79.) The warmth of the atmosphere offers of itself a very manifest advantage. The patients need not be shut up from cold, but can have all the benefit of life in the open air. Kingston is so dry and mild, and withal so healthy, that an aged friend, who has suffered much from rheumatism elsewhere, has not had a touch of it during a residence of 9 years in that city.

In addition to this climate, Jamaica possesses several most valuable medicinal springs. We merely name these—(1) The Bath of St. Thomas, a sulphurous, sodic, calcic spring, with a temperature of 130°; (2) The Milk River bath in Vere, a saline spring of 92° ; (3) The Jamaica Spa, a chalybeate (acidulous ferro-aluminous) spring, amid the finest mountain scenery, 3,000 feet up, 15 miles from Kingston, possesses almost the same qualities as the chalybeates of Spain, Belgium, which attract 16,000 visitors annually, and from which the Belgian Government derives a yearly revenue of more than £20,000.

Regarding these and other medicinal waters of Jamaica, we earnestly commend to the reader Dr. Phillippo's lecture of May 3, 1881, published by Messrs. Geo. Henderson & Co., Kingston, Jamaica, considering that it would be presumptuous to do anything else, as this is the newest and the fullest statement on this important subject, by one altogether competent to handle it.

Most confidently, therefore, and honestly does Jamaica invite to her shores those who suffer from forms of disease that are so difficult to deal with in the climates of the north.

II.—JAMAICA AS A PLACE TO SETTLE IN.

While Jamaica has not vacant areas of vast extent to offer to settlers, and while it is only in favourable circumstances that Europeans can labour under a vertical sun, yet Jamaica has tracts where not a few of such settlers could make for themselves a home, and the acquisition of them would be a real gain to the island. Men such as I have seen, with the spade, turn a bleak Scottish moorland into a cornfield, are gold to any land. Their industry and intelligence, their frugality, and home and social virtues could thrive here and surround them with comfort. Elevation about the sea-level secures the degree of coolness in which Europeans, beginning early and resting at noon, can do a fair day's work. Suppose medical help attainable at very moderate charge, and the means of moral and intellectual culture—the Church and School—easily accessible, and fair protection against plunderers afforded, in a good location, with good roads, securing access to a market for their produce, healthy European settlers could do fairly well for themselves and their offspring. But they must be of superior calibre, sober, intelligent, industrious, thrifty, and capable of more than one kind of industry. A man that settles on virgin land should know how to provide himself with a variety of things which, in other circumstances, he could purchase. The intervals of labour, when he should avoid exposure to the sun, would afford an ingenious man the time to produce things he needs, and even could sell. This is the kind of settler—of those dependent on their hands' work—who would most benefit Jamaica—such men as Samuel Laing describes in his "Journal of a residence in Norway in 1834-36"—the proprietor-peasantry of that country who "build their own houses, make their own chairs, tables, ploughs, carts, harness, iron-work, basket-work, and wood-work; in short, except window-glass, cast-iron ware, and pottery, everything about their houses and furniture is of their own fabrication" (c. ix.). And that such can do well and live in fair comfort, and even accumulate savings, is proved by the experience of those Germans and others who are settled in the higher parts of the parishes of Clarendon, St. Ann, and Manchester. Jamaica should try to attract such well-selected immigrants, and do all that can be done to give them a fair start.

Another class to whom Jamaica offers a fair field are men with some capital, who could hire and manage the labour of others ; men with the taste, habits, and intelligence for the cultivation and preparation of our marketable produce. Beyond question much of the produce of this island is absolutely wasted through sheer ignorance, as to the proper mode of curing and preparing it for the markets of the world, on the part of many; and on the part of many others, not so ignorant, through an utter lack of ambition, so they can get quit of their produce in any condition for a little ready money, to place it in the market in the finest condition possible. Jamaica has suffered, is suffering, and will suffer still more in all her industries from this soulless and unprincipled Africanism, every kind of antidote to which should earnestly be sought.

One great difficulty in the way of this second class of settlers, we shall be told, is that labour is not to be had. In old days new lands were brought under culture by means of slave labour. But is not our native population bound to increase, and would it not grow faster under better social and moral conditions? A foul moral atmosphere, vicious living, and the lack of amenities and helps tend greatly to prevent the increase of populati n. An immoral community never was, never can be, genuinely prolific, because, among such, those virtues are blasted that are necessary for the care and nurture of a healthy offspring. These can be secured for that weakest of terrestrial creatures—the human infant—only by virtuous family life. Existing and future proprietors and cultivators must seek to draw around them the best of the labouring class, and settle them on their properties in fair comfort, securing them a living, and thus also commanding their services at all times. A property cultivated by such hands is a far finer thing, is more natural and more satisfactory, than one that depends on gangs of foreign heathens. Beyond all question this island has within its borders, in soil, climate, and capacity, in the abundance of its harbours, in its nearness to the best markets of the world, and also, and not least, in the abundance of its native bone and sinew—men and women whose home and destiny are the torrid zone, the elements of all the social comforts and all the moderate prosperity that man needs in any part of the world. If we had men of a high tone determined, by God's help, to grasp and mould the advantages we possess, this island would in all important matters be the sunny land it is in climate and in beauty.

There are two classes whose settlement here would be a benefit to themselves and to this island :—

1. Sober, industrious, frugal, and intelligent workmen, skilled in earth-culture and in the various handicrafts, and such should be located on the most liberal terms and in the most favourable circumstances.

2. Men of some capital, who should make it their business to rear and cure the various marketable products of the island.

And now with regard to the lands which we hope to offer such settlers. In the Jamaica Blue-Book for 1877, it is stated that there are in the hands of the Government 90,000 acres, a large part of which lies in the Northern district of St. Thomas, and in the Southern parts of Portland—virgin land, well-watered, 2,000 to 6,000 feet above the sea, with a healthy climate, where Europeans can labour in the open air, and which are the finest areas for coffee and cinchona. There are also fine tracts in other parts of the island.

Besides these virgin lands, there are other lands in the possession of the Government for sale or lease, and also many properties in various parts of the island that may be obtained on favourable terms.

Means should be taken to furnish reliable information in Britain and America regarding the lands in Jamaica that await the settler—information so full, so accurate, and so true, that none shall be misled, but that the right class of men may have their attention arrested, and be enabled to form a correct judgment. And efforts should be made to place settlers of the first class in larger or smaller groups in the same neighbourhood, for mutual help and encouragement, and so that the means of preserving their intellectual and moral life, on which all depends for real and permanent success, may the more easily be maintained in their midst.

D.—CLIMATE OF THE SANTA CRUZ MOUNTAINS.

By JAMES HENRY CLARK, M.R.C.P., &c. &c.

A momentary enthusiasm often leads one to undertake duties the real difficulties of which are only discovered when the time approaches, and the hour has actually arrived for the fulfilment of our undertaking.

As a busy practitioner beset with many difficulties, in a large country district, I find the preparation of a Paper on the climate of the Santa Cruz Mountains no easy task ; but I owe a debt of gratitude to the climate myself, and, after 14 years' practice in this island, invalids are entitled to my experience ; accept, therefore, the tribute, such as it is, not for the deed, but for the will.

The Santa Cruz Mountains, situated in the parish of St. Elizabeth, " extend from Yardley Chase on the seacoast, to Lacovia Bridge. The crest of the ridge runs from Corby Castle, through Potsdam, Torrington, and Malvern, to Stanmore Hill ; from the latter place, it decreases gradually in height until it finally terminates abruptly at an altitude less than one-half the greatest elevation," which is at Potsdam Endowed School, 2,500 feet.

The geological formation is chiefly " white limestone, with a thick coating of red ferruginous earth."

The red soil above the white limestone is extremely productive, and it is upon this that coffee is grown.

Change of air and scene, especially pure air and exercise, are beneficial not only to the invalid—affording pleasurable excitement of mind, withdrawing the attention from bodily ailments, and dissipating gloomy forebodings—but to those tourists who, having means, are in search of a health climate for a home ; where, without exposure to malarious influences, a life of comfort and leisure may be led. For all such the climate in these mountains will be found perfect.

To any anxious to avoid a winter, or who, suffering from a tendency to

G

bronchitis, inflammation of the lungs, pleurisy, rheumatism, or dyspepsia, must in a variable and chilly climate, though not labouring under advanced disease, be confined to the house during a large portion of the year, to avoid the almost certainty of "taking cold." To all such persons I do most conscientiously recommend this climate. Here the invalid can get out every day to enjoy those most powerful of all tonics—fresh air and exercise ; and thus, by promoting appetite and digestion, impart vigour and tone to the general system.

This could not possibly be done "at home."

"A Hypothetical Consumptive Atlantis," says Richardson, "should be near the seacoast and sheltered from north winds. The soil should be dry, the drinking-water pure, the temperature about 60°, with an average of not more than 10° to 15° on either side."

All authorities agree that mountain air is of great importance in treating diseases of the chest, and that the best climates for the majority of consumptive invalids are those which are warm, dry, and equable.

From observations very kindly recorded for me at the Potsdam Endowed Schools, I find that—

The average annual maximum temperature was . 75·3°
,,   ,,   ,,   minimum   ,,   ,, . 66·8°
,,   ,,   ,,   mean   ,,   ,, . 71·1°

That the rainfall for the year 1888 was 38·25 inches—rainy days, 91.

This temperature and rainfall correspond very closely with Algiers, in the northern part of Africa, much resorted to by invalids.

In Algiers the rainfall is 36 inches. The number of rainy days, 96.

The mean annual temperature .   .   .   . 66·50°
,,   ,, temperature for Spring   .   .   . 68·60°
,,   ,,   ,,   ,, Summer .   .   . 77·78°
,,   ,,   ,,   ,, Autumn .   .   . 63·80°

The climate of Algiers, and, as I believe, of the Santa Cruz Mountains also, may be said to be opposed to the generation, as well as to the evolution of tubercle in the lungs. Europeans who do not bring the germ of the disease to Algiers almost never become phthisical. Those who do bring not only a predisposition, but actually crude tubercle, in greater or less quantity in the lung are often cured ; or, in the worst cases, the progress of the disease is extremely slow.

I am acquainted with a gentleman whose mother suffered from lung disease and died ; he spat blood on two occasions before leaving Europe in 1844 for the West Indies ; he is still living, and attributes this to climate and care.

Many cases have come under my observation, where persons having a tendency to consumption, or after inflammation of the lungs, left England for this country, and by prolonged residence have been practically cured.

During the 14 years I have been in practice no death from fever has occurred. Yellow fever is unknown, and only 1 case of typhoid—

ending in recovery—has been treated. This fever has not its origin here, but was brought from a seaport town.

One year I had on my visiting list 7 Europeans and 2 natives, whose ages added together amounted to 751 years.

But, it will be asked, "How can we get to this mountain? Where can we lodge? What can we see?" Tourists and invalids from Kingston can travel either by rail and coach to Mandeville, hiring a conveyance thence to the Santa Cruz Mountains, or by coasting steamer to Black River, and hiring a conveyance at this seaport, after a pleasant drive of two or three hours, be located in very comfortable lodgings on the mountain top.

It would be advisable always to engage rooms before coming, and I should recommend intending visitors to communicate by letter, stating full particulars, addressed to "The Postmistress at Malvern P. O." This lady will, I am sure, supply information as to rooms, residences, charges.

The roads are in excellent order, so that carriage drives may be enjoyed.

There is a large market at Malvern twice a week, where the delicious fruits of this country, and occasionally grapes, can be procured, with vegetables, beef, and mutton; fresh fish can be obtained three times a week.

The Post-Office is accessible, mails arrive and are despatched three times a week, and a Telegraph Office is within 8 miles.

Two churches and a Moravian chapel are open on Sundays for Divine Service.

Parents or guardians of delicate children, or persons who are in search of a good climate for some member of the family, will be within easy reach of the Potsdam Endowed School for Boys, the head-master of which is a Cambridge M.A. (classical honours). There is also an Endowed School for Girls, which will soon be presided over by a lady from England.

It will thus be seen that ample and unusual educational advantages are to be found in addition to climate.

But the invalids ask: "What can I see?" There are few spots on earth where natural beauties so combine with those of man's creation to please and interest him. The beauties of nature abound on every side, and to persons who sketch, or paint, there is plenty to amuse and edify; but invalids must not be encouraged to undergo fatigue and exposure in "sight seeing"; crowded and heated rooms, late hours, all operate injuriously, and destroy entirely the beneficial influences of climate.

It is absolutely necessary for invalids to bear in mind that the climate must be regarded merely as the change placing them in the most favourable position for the removal of disease; that advice should be taken and followed as to diet and exercise; and "that," in the words of Sir James Clarke on climate, "if in some points greater latitude may be allowed, others will demand even a more rigid attention; and that it is only by a due regard to all these circumstances, that the powers of the constitution can be enabled to throw off or even materially mitigate, in the best climate, a disease of long standing."

E.–THE CLIMATE OF THE HILLS OF THE PARISH OF MANCHESTER.

By the Rev. H. WALDER, Moravian Missionary.

I am convinced the Manchester hills here may be ranked alongside the healthiest places in England or on the Continent of Europe. My parents, who lived all their lives in Switzerland (Canton Zürich), came here about eight years ago, and have ever since enjoyed better health than in their native country. My father, who is of a very delicate constitution, is now, in his seventy-sixth year, all the day on his legs in the open air.

The climate at Mizpah, where we reside, is all that can be desired.

Mizpah is about 2,400 feet above the sea, nearly 1,300 feet above Shooter's Hill P. O., and within half a mile of Spitzbergen, which Sawkins gives at 2,514 feet. We have neither the summer heat of Europe, of America, nor their winter's cold. The thermometer ranges between 64° to 80° in the shade. Easterly winds are prevalent and very frequent. On the west we have the Mile Gully Mountain Range; on the east the Clarendon Mountains; to the south we see Carlisle Bay in clear weather.

We have passing fogs after heavy showers in the lowlands to the south, and the atmosphere is rather damp, especially in the rainy season, but, for all that, the climate is most salubrious, as proved by the following statistics collected from the church books of the small Mizpah congregation (average 473 souls) during the years 1870-81 inclusive. During these twelve (11¾) years, we have had 60 deaths, and, during the same period, 241 baptisms, which prove the death-rate in this congregation to have been only about one-fourth of the birth-rate during the period in question.

Of the 60 persons who died, 1 is entered at about 100 years old, 7 are entered as between 80 and 90 years old, 17 had reached man's allotted term of threescore years and ten; of 6 the age is given as 60, 4 died from accidents, 10 died as infants; of 4 fever is entered as the cause of death.

Some fall victims to diarrhœa every year, but, when considering the impure water which many people have to drink, especially during seasons of drought, which occur in this parish almost every year, and how many people, in times of scarcity, have to subsist on unripe yams and fruit, the wonder is that so comparatively few succumb to bowel complaints.

Taking furthermore into consideration the innumerable wettings which the generality of the people are exposed to, without even being able to put on a dry suit, and, in addition, the very great defects in the homes of the peasantry, in a sanitary point of view, it cannot be denied that the above facts speak loudly in praise of the climate in these districts.

I may add that I am able to state from personal observation that the ordinary diseases of children appear here in a much milder form than is the case of Europe.

COLONIAL AND INDIAN EXHIBITION.

THE WEST INDIES.

Extracted from the Times *of Friday, August 20, 1886.*

Coming to the West Indies proper, one naturally turns to Jamaica as the largest and most important of our colonies in this group. Its area, 4,200 square miles, is about one-third, and its population, 580,000, is somewhat less than one-half of the area and population of the whole group. It has been in our possession for 230 years. This island (to which Turks and Caicos islands, 170 square miles, are attached), like Trinidad and Barbados, forms an independent colony. All the other islands are grouped under two governments or collective colonies—(1) Leeward Islands, including Antigua, Montserrat, St. Kitts, Nevis, Dominica, and the Virgin Islands; (2) Windward Islands, including Grenada, St. Vincent, Tobago, St. Lucia; while the Bahamas form a multitudinous and complicated group of reefs by themselves away on the western verge of the Atlantic.

Jamaica, lying in the bosom of the Caribbean Sea, sheltered north and east by Cuba and Hayti, may be taken in its history as a typical West India island. Although comparatively early in its career it was granted a certain amount of self-government, still, like most of the other islands and our old colonies elsewhere, it was regarded until well on into the last century as existing solely for the benefit of the mother country. Still, in spite of vexatious ordinances and taxation, it prospered, and many a fortune was made out of it. For nearly two centuries its prosperity was founded on slavery, and when 53 years ago that institution was abolished throughout the British dominions, social and industrial disorganization was the result; estates ran to waste, the black population became demoralised, industry lapsed, and commerce declined. This was to be expected, but it was a state of things that time would remedy, and time has done so to a great extent. So helpless had the whites become that they prayed the home Government to withdraw their Constitution and treat the island as a Crown colony. It is a hopeful sign that a year or two ago the old Constitution was to a considerable extent restored. Education has done its work, and in Jamaica, as in other West India islands, there are coloured and black subjects of Her Majesty as prosperous as any white colonist, and whose manners cannot be distinguished from those of an English gentleman. It is now thought by many who abhor slavery that its sudden abolition was an ill-considered step; but that is ground which we need not go into here. We are well rid of it, even at the price it has cost us. All would have been going well had it not been for the check to the sugar industry, to which we have already referred. Still, that the island has not recovered from the results of slavery is seen in the fact that in the year 1838 (the year of emancipation) the value of the sugar, rum, and coffee exported was £1,500,000; in 1885 it was only £900,000. This, however, is partly due to the decline in price of all these articles. In 1874, for example, we find that 92,000 cwt. of coffee brought £337,000, while in 1885 80,650 cwt. brought only £157,000. In

1874 1,935,000 gallons of rum brought £290,000, whereas in 1885 2,000,000 gallons realised only £284,000. In 1874 for 511,000 cwt. of sugar £483,000 were paid ; in 1885 500,000 cwt. realised only £307,800. But Jamaica is not in nearly so bad case as other West India islands; for though sugar is important, there are other staples not far behind it, and new cultures are rapidly obtaining an important place in the exports. Though sugar has declined, Jamaica rum still holds its old high place among all the rums of the world. In 1885, while sugar formed 22 per cent. of the exports, rum counted 17 per cent., coffee, fruits, and dyewood 11 per cent. each. Fruit especially is rapidly rising in importance—bananas, oranges, pine-apples, especially, and also limes and mangoes. Bananas alone were exported in 1884 to the value of £192,000 ; in 1874 only £6,350 worth were exported. Oranges grew from £3,386 in 1874 to £58,295 in 1884 ; 1885 was a bad year for everything. While Jamaica takes about half her imports from the United Kingdom, she sends her only about one-third of her exports, her principal customer being the United States. Among other articles which figure for substantial sums in the exports of Jamaica are cocoa-nuts, beeswax, ginger, hides, pimento, yams, and walking-sticks. So that after all, if sugar should fail her, she has plenty of other resources to fall back upon. Still, for ten years there has been no increase in either exports or imports, and but little for the last 20 years. And yet there is ample room for enterprise in the island. Less than one-fourth of the total area is under cultivation ; there are upwards of 1,800,000 acres available for agricultural and pastoral purposes. Of the total population only 14,400 are whites ; 110,000 are " coloured " (i.e., mixed), while 444,000 are blacks. But it is difficult to induce these blacks to work as they ought, and there has been a large coolie immigration. There are 11,000 coolies in the island. Here, as in most of the other islands, both labour and capital are wanted ; for the latter there is ample scope, and no white man need be afraid of the climate. But capital without labour is useless, and for the labour difficulty it is not easy to suggest a solution. The growth of steady, industrious habits on the part of the negroes is essential to the prosperity of Jamaica, and it is in this view that the cultivation of fruit and preserves should be strongly encouraged. Still for the cane fields a good Chinese labourer is the best that can be obtained.

In the Jamaica Court all the products are well represented, thanks mainly to the liberality and energy of Mr. Washington Eves, the Honorary Commissioner. There are 20 samples of sugar of various kinds—vacuum pan, centrifugal, and Muscovado. But rum entirely eclipses sugar so far as the number of samples is concerned. There are about 90 samples, mostly of crops 1885 and 1886, though some specimens of merchants' rum are from ten to thirty years old. There are also many samples of liqueurs and cordials, such as rum shrub, orange spirit, pimento dram, cashew wine, bitters, noyeau, &c. The fruits of the island do not seem to be so well represented as they might have been, which may arise from the fact that much has yet to be learnt as to methods of packing. There are no pine-apples, for example, though we have mangoes, cashews, alligator pears, nutmegs, and a few other things. The cocoa-nut palm is fairly represented in fruit and manufactured products. There is a very large show of coffee, about 70 samples, including a specimen or two of Liberia coffee, which seems to be still in the experimental stage. This coffee is well suited for the low country, requiring both less attention and labour than Arabian coffee. The Arabian coffee is largely cultivated in the mountain districts, especially the Blue Mountains, and for gentlemen with moderate capital and a taste for colonial life this is an industry which deserves consideration. We find about a dozen specimens of pimento (Jamaica pepper or allspice), the dried and cured berries of *Pimenta vulgaris*, a product of which Jamaica has almost the monopoly. There is considerable fluctuation in the export of this article ; its value in 1854 was £83,000, in 1884 £92,800, and in 1885 £53,860. The plant is highly remunerative in favourable years ; it grows without cultivation of any sort in ordinary pasture lands.

We find a good many samples of cacao in various stages, and this is a product which at one time promised to become the staple culture of Jamaica. Its culture is reviving, the number of plantations is on the increase, and if proper care is taken in the preparation of the article it ought to figure largely in future years among the exports. Annatto seeds, used for colouring purposes, and yielding a fair return, are well represented. Cinchona is still in the experimental stage, though Mr. Morris, now of Kew, has done much to foster its cultivation in the higher lands. There is a fair number of specimens in the Exhibition which look satisfactory. For settlers who can afford to await the growth of the trees for interest on their capital, Jamaica presents many advantages for cinchona culture. At the same time it must be remembered that the cultivation of cinchona has so largely increased in tropical countries, and especially in India, that the high value once realised by this article can no longer be obtained. While on this subject we may express our surprise that no Government botanist has been appointed to succeed Mr. D. Morris ; surely this is a penny-wise and pound-foolish policy. The court contains exhibits of many other medicinal and economic substances, essential oils, perfumes, and odds and ends like beeswax (an important export), honey, meals, starches, &c., all of which deserve attention, and are capable of developments as colonial resources. Of tobacco there are a few samples in the shape of cigars, and a few years ago Jamaica cigars found a place in the London market ; but they do not seem to have taken. Perhaps their sale at the stalls in the Exhibition may increase the demand. We have a sample or two of tea, a culture only in the experimental stage ; but with the sample of Ceylon's success before it, and with the great variety of climate in the colony, it is quite worth carrying out a thorough series of experiments. If tea could become fairly established as a Jamaica industry, the future of the colony would be made.

There are about twenty exhibits of fibres in this court, but although Jamaica possesses many fibre-yielding plants, it is not yet clear whether any can be turned to economical use. Experiments with machinery of various kinds have been conducted for some time, and it is to be hoped that the general result will be favourable. Silk grass, bowstring hemps, and China grass are among the most abundant of these fibres. Some 250 samples of wood are exhibited ; including a few specimens of logwood, by far the most important timber of the colony commercially. Ebony, fustic, and lignum vitæ are the only other wood exports of any extent, the fact being that Jamaica has no large forests. Still, as the specimens shown in the Exhibition prove, there are some extremely beautiful cabinet and furniture woods in the colony of which surely something could be made under competent guidance.

The court contains a very great variety of fancy articles, interesting as showing in what directions the smaller industries may be developed among the people. A good many of these are exhibited by the Jamaica Women's Self-help Society and the Governors of the Jamaica Institution. These find favour with visitors, and a considerable business has been done in them. Many of them exhibit great taste and ingenuity. Nor must we forget the collection of walking-sticks, an export of some importance, and the bamboos so abundant in Jamaica. The oil-paintings showing Jamaica in past times are extremely interesting, and the larger and finer collection of photographs deserves particular mention. There is no educational exhibit in this court, partly, no doubt, because there is no Government system of education, the various denominations doing pretty well all that is wanted. There are, however, three Government training colleges. Altogether, the Jamaica Court presents a very fair picture of the varied industries and interests of the colony, and it may be hoped that a proper development of its resources will make the present depression in no long time a matter of history. All the necessary information on points of interest to intending settlers can be obtained from the Jamaica Government direct, or from the Honorary Commissioner in the court, Mr. C. Washington Eves.

Spottiswoode & Co. Printers, New-street Square, London.

www.ingramcontent.com/pod-product-compliance
Lightning Source LLC
Chambersburg PA
CBHW020758020726
47495CB00008B/2489